BETHANY'S JUSTICE

When Bethany walks with her friend, Kezzie, to the neighbouring fair, she has no way of knowing that their journey will lead to peril and humiliation. Her friend's infatuation with Bill Judd nearly causes the fall of both young women. Abandoned by Kezzie, Bethany has no notion that the road she now treads will lead her beyond the reach of a family like the Judd's and into the lives of Richard and Bartholomew; who are two very different brothers.

Books by Valerie Holmes
in the Linford Romance Library:

THE MASTER OF
MONKTON MANOR
THE KINDLY LIGHT
HANNAH OF HARPHAM HALL
PHOEBE'S CHALLENGE
BETRAYAL OF INNOCENCE
AMELIA'S KNIGHT
OBERON'S CHILD
REBECCA'S REVENGE
THE CAPTAIN'S CREEK
MISS GEORGINA'S CURE
CALEB'S FAITH
THE SEABRIGHT SHADOWS
A STRANGER'S LOVE
HEART AND SOUL

VALERIE HOLMES

BETHANY'S JUSTICE

Complete and Unabridged

LINFORD
Leicester

First published in Great Britain in 2008

First Linford Edition
published 2008

British Library CIP Data

Holmes, Valerie
Bethany's justice.—Large print ed.—
Linford romance library
1. Love stories
2. Large type books
I. Title
823.9′2 [F]

ISBN 978–1–84782–413-

Published by
F. A. Thorpe (Publishing)
Anstey, Leicestershire

Set by Words & Graphics Ltd.
Anstey, Leicestershire
Printed and bound in Great Britain by
T. J. International Ltd., Padstow, Cornwall

This book is printed on acid-free paper

1

Bethany busied herself clearing away what was left of the freshly baked loaf from the old oak table. She was so excited at the thought of where she was going today that her hand was already shaking. She stacked the pewter plates up in the stone basin and poured in some water from the jug.

'Now then, lass, you take care how you go along that road, especially through the woods. Honestly, you hear so many tales of what folks get up to that you just don't know what's right and what's wrong. Mind you, there's no smoke without a fire or a bit of kindling, that's for sure.'

Isadora patted the girl's back, 'Don't you come walking back over the moor in the dark. You must give yerself plenty of time in the daylight. It gets dreadful cold up there and dangerous of a night, not as safe as in the vale. If any of them farm hands gets a bit friendly, you give them a sharp slap and tell them Isadora Hawk will be after their blood if they don't act like gents.'

She shook her head. 'They act badly enough, does the gentry. Money doesn't make a man good.'

Isadora Hawk had her shawl on ready to leave the cottage and start her walk to the poor-house where she helped out with the children for a small remuneration. She stopped by the threshold and looked at Bethany and sighed.

'Lass, you'll cost me an ear-wiggin' from Mister Littleboy, but I can't bear to see yer fumblin' round like that, all fingers and thumbs. Get yersel' off to the fair, stay together. You and Kezzie Root need to be close as company in order to safeguard the other, and don't come home late or it'll be the last time you'll be given the chance to go a roamin'.' Isadora blushed as Bethany hugged her and kissed the woman's cheek.

Isadora was not one for great outbursts

of affection, having lived by her husband, James', more sombre approach to life. But Bethany knew they were both good people because they had taken her in as a baby abandoned on the doorstep of the poor-house. Isadora had taken her home rather than see her placed with the other unwanted orphans.

Isadora put down her shawl on the back of the chairs, washed the plates and cleared the table, placing the chairs back neatly. James liked order and could not abide a dirty or unruly home. It may have been small and humble, but Isadora took great care and pride in her little cottage.

Bethany almost ran up the ladder that took her to her own cot in the roof space, her bedchamber away from the three sons who also shared the cottage with Isadora and James.

The reason for her excitement today was market day — here at last. Bethany was so excited. Today, she would put on her finest hat, her only hat in fact, her newly darned shawl, and wear her polished boots; if the leather held together at least until she could make it to the cobbler's in the town. She felt as if she was dressed fit for church and to mix with the moneyed folk.

She had brushed out her thick hair and swept it up on to her head. She had no curls as was the fashion, so tucked all her hair neatly into a bun, before the hat had been carefully positioned.

This was no ordinary market day, just for the selling of the sheep's wool, or the cows' and horse flesh. No, this was going to be a fair in celebration of the new owners of the land. No-one knew much about them, but their son had returned from the war, a lieutenant and, from the word around he was a hero, too. So everyone was to celebrate — except folk like Isadora who had to attend to the poor.

Mind, Bethany thought with a smile, even they were going to have a special dinner today, after they've bathed and received a new outfit of clothes from the Ruddingtons. Imagine, she thought, being given new clothes.

As Bethany wrapped her shawl around her she pictured in her mind what the festivities would be like; there would be traders, bakers and jugglers. The whole village would go there, so would their neighbouring farmers. But the real reason why she was so eager to go this year was that she would be able to see Bill once more. She had seen him three times in church and each time he had looked at her, discreetly.

The last time he was so bold that he even dared to wink at her when no other person could notice. It was a moment that had marked her heart and set her apart from the other girls there. He was known to have an eye for a pretty girl. Isadora had said that many times, but Kezzie knew his family and said that he was a real gentle giant. Beth ran back down the ladder jumping off the last two steps and landing firmly in front of a disapproving Isadora.

'Lass, get yerself out of here and make the most of the day. They don't come round often, but Bethany, take care. You get in trouble and I'll not hear the end of it from your pa.'

'I will, honest. Bye, Ma. Enjoy your meal.' Bethany ran out of the cottage and up the street, bidding folk good morning as she rushed past them. Some were already on their way. Others had burdens to carry, goods to sell or skills to trade. She saw Kezzie up ahead, sitting on a milestone at the side of the road. Her hair was full of curls and yellow like the sun, Bethany often thought in her more fanciful moments.

Kezzie was friendly, everyone seemed to like her and she knew so many more people than Bethany herself did. She'd worked up at the big house as a maid with the old family. But all the staff had been sent home when the old dowager died the previous year. Then the house had fallen into a deserted, silent state, dust covers hiding what had at one time been proudly displayed to the dowager's few visitors. Now the new owners had arrived, bringing most of their own people with them. Kezzie could stay at home and help her ma when she could be found, for the girl liked her freedom.

'Beth, you decided to come. I was just about to set off on my own,' Kezzie said, as she greeted her friend with a hug and, although Bethany knew that Isadora did not share her enthusiasm for the girl's character, Beth loved her because she made her feel happy.

'I said I would, but I had some chores to finish off first.' The girls fell into step with each other, linking arms as they walked along.

'That Isadora works you like a scullery maid. You should stand up for yourself.'! Kezzie exclaimed. 'Being the only girl there you should be pampered not worked like a skivvy.' She felt the palm of Bethany's hand.

'Give over, Kezzie. I only do my fair share.' Bethany was fiercely protective of Isadora. She had cared for her all her life and Beth loved her dearly; most of the time she was pleased to help out. She quickly changed the subject to one that she knew would take Kezzie's attention from her own family. 'You've a new piece of ribbon in your bonnet; so pretty a blue, it matches your eyes, Kez.'

Her ma seemed to always find some little thing that would make Kezzie shine out from the crowd.

'Do you like it?' She turned her head this way and that so that her curls bounced slightly.

'Yes, I do . . . tell me, do you think that Bill Judd will be there, showing off his sheep? Flash, his dog, is the best around; I think he'll win the competition, don't you?'

Kezzie giggled impishly.

'I suspect he'll be showing something off,' she winked at Bethany, 'he's proper proud of himself is Bill.'

Bethany laughed. 'You're wicked, Kezzie, but I suppose he is very confident. I wonder why he hasn't found himself a wife by now. He must be at least four years older than us,' Bethany said aloud what she was thinking, but wished she hadn't when she saw Kezzie's face take a much more serious expression.

'You sound as if you have some idea as to who he should be thinking about . . . you perhaps?' She had tilted her head on one side and was staring at Bethany, who immediately blushed.

'Me! No, that wasn't what I meant. I was just thinking that's all.' Bethany forced a smile.

'Good, because you mustn't wed, my dear friend, or our trips will end. You'll spend all your time raising brats and feeding a man up until he's plump as Isadora's James. So come. Let's run and have some fun. We want to be first there and last to leave. Race you there!'

Bethany saw her run, lifting her skirts immorally high to keep it from the dirt. Reluctantly, Bethany followed hoping her boots would not split under the pressure.

She was glad Kezzie had not taken her words seriously, but if Bill even noticed her at the fair, Bethany knew her day would be complete.

2

Breathlessly they paused from their run and together they climbed up along the forested road, dappled as it was by the bright spring sunshine. The moor was a stark contrast as they arrived at the top of the bank. They leaned against a milestone and watched as a cart went past, laden with goods for the fair. From here they only needed to walk a further half mile on the flat before descending into the neighbouring vale, where all would be a hive of activity as the people amassed for the fair.

'Oh, this will be so fine, I wonder if many of the local gentry will be there. Surely, they must be. Oh, to see them sitting in their fine coaches. Oh, I should have been born one. I would set the season in London alight!'

Bethany watched her friend spin around gracefully on the toe of her boot and finish in a deep and graceful curtsey.

'You have such notions, Kezzie! How will you ever settle down to a normal life?' Bethany asked as she approached her flamboyant friend.

'I have no intention of 'settling down' to this life! I shall meet a handsome rich gentleman at the fair and I will sweep him off his feet with my charm.' She giggled at the thought whilst Beth shook her head at the girl's outrageous ideas. 'Here, Bethany, help me to fix my hair. I rather foolishly forgot my composure as we ran amok!' Kezzie held out a comb which she had kept hidden in her skirts.

Bethany took it from her and dutifully fixed her friend's hair. It never failed to amuse and amaze Bethany how the girl could be like one of her brothers one minute, active and quite common in her conversation, and then when she sniffed the air and knew that moneyed people were near, she changed her deportment and persona. She imagined herself one of them ever since she worked in the large house.

'Your trouble, Bethany, is that you have no imagination. You can't see yourself beyond the chores that Isadora has you 'dutifully' performing. You're like one of the sheep in the flock, not daring to go beyond the group, but I'm like Flash, the sheep dog.'

Bethany laughed and could see that this reaction was not what Kezzie had wanted or expected from her friend. 'Does that make you much better? It means that whoever the shepherd is has you at his beck and call!'

Bethany's attention had already been taken by the figure approaching over the moor trod, the old trails that criss-crossed the moors. She was unaware of the cold expression that had settled on to Kezzie's face. 'Look, Kez, it's Bill Judd!' Bethany pointed up ahead of them with the comb still in her hand.

Bethany tried to compose herself. She didn't want to appear foolish in front of either of them, particularly Bill.

At once Kezzie's attention was fixed on the tall, broad shouldered frame who was making his way down from the moor towards them.

Kezzie placed her hand on the comb, but Bethany did not lose her grip on it. 'Kez, can I use it? My hair is an unruly mess too,' Bethany asked quickly. Bill was only about twenty paces away from them.

Kezzie glanced at him, snatched the comb out of Bethany's hand and slipped it into her pocket. 'Don't be silly, Beth! Yours always slips out anyway. You know it is always in a state so don't fuss about it now. Besides, you don't want Bill seeing you combing it in front of him, do you? He'll think you're after him for sure.'

Kezzie's pale blue eyes appeared to represent ice to Bethany as the girl glanced at her, before turning her back to greet Bill with a sweet smile. If she knew how much her action and words had affected Bethany's mood and confidence she gave no sign of it.

Bethany discreetly tucked a few long dark brown strands of hair up into her bonnet.

Bill was only two paces away when Kezzie took a step away from Bethany and stared at the ground where the girl was standing. She glanced downwards, shaking her head and said rather loudly, 'Good gracious, Bethany, cannot Isadora afford to at least mend your old boots, or are you to walk about barefoot!'

Bethany looked down, and for the first time realised to her horror that her boot had a split the size of her little finger by the sole; revealing the darned toe of her stocking. Beth was still studying it, appalled and filled with embarrassment at both the state of the boot and her friend's loud deliverance of her comments; her cheeks flushed red with shame as Bill greeted them.

'Can I join you, ladies?' he asked, as he swung his walking stick casually by his side. 'We appear to be goin' the same way.' He winked at Kezzie and touched a finger to his cap as he looked at Beth.

'Of course you can, Bill,' Kezzie answered, 'but I don't know if 'we' are continuing to the fair.'

'Whyever not?' he asked, as if the notion that they were not was highly unlikely.

'Well, Bethany may not be able to.' Kezzie leaned closer to him and said quietly, 'Her boot has split. She can hardly hobble around on it all day long now can she?'

Bill squatted near Bethany's foot.

Bethany fidgeted uneasily. 'Really, there is no need to fuss. I shall go to the fair and see if there is a cobbler who can fix it.'

'Oh, and with what will you pay him, Beth? You really should go back and tell that Isadora how she has ruined your day. You may be a child still, but it is time she learned to treat you with more consideration.'

Kezzie's words stung Bethany, but it was the closeness of Bill as he placed one strong hand around her ankle, lifting the boot slightly to study the slit that made her feel strange.

She watched the top of his head, trying to control what she was feeling. She should be ashamed, but her senses were so confused. He was actually holding a part of her. His dark brown eyes looked up into hers. 'Bethany, we can make a quick fix until you can get it seen to.' He untied a piece of leather from around his stick and quickly bound it around the toe of her boot. She glanced up at Kezzie who was standing with her arms folded and a grim expression on her face.

'Try that,' Bill said, as he stood up again.

'That's much better,' Bethany replied shyly as she placed it down on the ground again. She smiled at him, with a genuine warmth, and gratitude.

'Good, that should see you safely back home. Don't worry about Kezzie, I'll see she's safe.' He tipped another finger at his hat and turned around and started talking and chatting to Kezzie.

Bethany felt as though she had been dismissed. He whistled, and Flash came running from over the moor to fall in at the side of his master.

Kezzie waved as they walked off together. 'Don't worry about me, Bethany, I'll bring you a treat back.'

Bethany stood there, her fists clenched at her side, tears of frustration welling up in her eyes, but neither Bill nor Kezzie glanced back at her.

It was some minutes before she moved. More people passed her by. Some of them were on foot, some on carts, wagons or in gigs. The world was moving about her, determined to have their share of fun, but hers had stopped still. Something inside her ignited like a flame.

She wiped her eyes with the back of her hand. She was not a child! Kezzie had no right to dictate to her what she did, said or where she went, neither did the big oaf, Bill Judd.

If he was such a selfish brute as to leave a young woman on her own to walk back down a lonely track, just so he could be with her friend — Bethany laughed at the word 'friend' — then she had been wrong about him. What he looked like on the outside betrayed what he was like underneath his handsome skin. Isadora had Kezzie's character pinned, but Bethany had been so foolish and gullible.

She looked up at the sun, shielding her eyes from its almighty power, and forced herself to smile. 'I shall go to the fair and I'll get there before them!' she said to herself before running to the top of the next vale. Over tree tops she could see the rings, the tents, the stalls and carriages all waiting for her to join them. She saw the road ahead of her. It lined the top of the vale, sun dappling the colours of the land either side.

In the far distance she could make out the figures of a man, a dog and a *girl*; she could never catch them up. Neither did she want to. No, there was another way; her brother had shown her it once when he had been late to meet a friend. She headed off the road and into the wooded bank.

The woods belonged to the dowager's house. So long as she was careful and did not slip, tearing her dress or muddying it then she would be there before them. The thought of seeing the look upon their faces as they entered to see her sitting waiting, drove her onwards. She collected up her skirt above knee height and held it firm in one hand whilst she steadied herself with the other, leaning her weight upon the trees as she picked her way down the steep slope.

It was darker in here, but her heart beat faster and she felt alive. It was only when something hit her head that she slowed. She swayed for a moment and sank to her knees.

Bethany placed her fingers on her brow and was surprised when she felt something warm and moist. Staring at her fingers she saw blood; she swayed slightly before looking upwards at the tree.

The splintered wood in the trunk confirmed what she had unbelievably suspected, a bullet had ripped through the air, grazing her forehead. She clung to the tree and stared around her. The birds had stopped singing, the air was still. She froze, barely believing her own thoughts. Someone had nearly killed her.

Bethany slowly clambered further down the slope, but she heard twigs breaking and bushes being pushed away behind her. Danger approached.

Scared, but determined to escape whatever madness she had stumbled into, she ran quickly across a short clearing and into the tall ferns at the other side.

Here in the dense undergrowth she huddled down close to the ground — waiting, watching every leaf that moved amongst the trees opposite. She prayed then, whoever *they* were, would assume she had run on, following the pathway back down towards the vale.

Her patience was rewarded as two

men, one carrying a gun, appeared from where she had entered the clearing. She stared, fearful, but without making a sound. Even her breath seemed heavy as she let it escape from her trembling body.

To her surprise both of the men were well dressed. The first even wore a uniform. He was the one with the gun in his hand. His hair was short and curly, rather like a girl's, she thought to herself.

'Bartholomew, you can not go around here taking pot-shots at anything that catches your eye! You are not fighting Napoleon anymore. If that bird, or whatever it was you winged back there, had been a local taking a short cut to the fair you could face serious charges. This cavalier attitude has to stop. Here, murder is murder — this is not a battle ground!' The taller and, Bethany suspected, the slightly younger of the two men reprimanded his companion.

'Richard, if that had been a local

villain I would be a hero all over again for taking the blackguard down! The local scum take liberties, trespassing on our land and even fishing in our river. It is time they learned to respect other people's property. I have fought long and hard for the price of liberty.' The fairer man of the two faced the other, his head held high — proud, the other had glanced down during Bartholomew's reply.

'You are really playing this hero role to the full, aren't you? Enjoying all the fuss and attention. Well do so whilst it lasts. People have expectations of heroes, Bartholomew, you may find such an unnatural role difficult to live up to.'

Richard fixed a stare at Bartholomew. His stance was casual, though, unlike that of the *hero* who seemed, to Bethany, the sort who was incapable of slouching or relaxing.

'Jealous are we, little brother? Never mind. You stay and play gamekeeper whilst I return, I have my public to meet.' Bartholomew threw the rifle at Richard, who caught it in one hand. 'Don't worry, little brother — it's not loaded, it won't go bang!' Bartholomew laughed, before looking around him.

He strode off down the path towards the manor house, but Richard stood stock still, with the rifle slung across his back, watching his brother leave.

Once he was out of sight, Bethany expected him to leave also, but instead he turned towards her hiding place. Standing one pace from where she was huddled he said calmly, 'Whoever you are, show yourself. You will not be harmed further.'

Bethany hesitated then realised there was no point in pretending she was not there. The man obviously knew she was. Carefully, and slowly, she stood up. Bethany saw the look of surprise upon Richard's face. He hadn't expected her, a woman, to appear.

She stepped out on to the path, but had not realised that the strapping on her boot had come loose and she stumbled on the sole as it hung down from her foot.

Richard instantly put out a hand to steady her, taking hers in his. It was then that he saw the line of blood on her forehead just near her hair line. 'You poor thing, you must be terrified! Here, we shall make all well.' Without asking her or consulting her, he swept her up in his arms and started to walk her along the path. He was strong, but she let out a squeal as her feet left the ground.

'Sir, unhand me, please. I . . . I . . . am supposed to be at the fair, and I . . . '

'Can hardly turn up looking like that! No, miss, you have been wronged and we shall make all well again. You were indeed fortunate that you have no more than a mere scratch upon your crown, but the shock of such an incident should not be ignored. Nor the damage to your boots and attire. This is bad of Bartholomew, but I hope that I can make amends for his accident. He has recently returned from the war, miss, and is used to life having a very different set of rules.'

He looked at her face and smiled as she blushed back. This was a whole new experience for her. Everything that had happened to her today was.

'He nearly killed me!' she said quietly.

'True, he could have done so, but miss, you were trespassing on our land and I'm afraid the fact he didn't kill you, you only had a superficial scratch, could easily be interpreted as a war hero's excellent skill at marksmanship, and that no more than a warning shot was ever intended.' He raised an eyebrow at her.

'Are you warning me, sir, not to make trouble?' Bethany felt quite cross as she felt she had every right to make a fuss about it.

'Not warning, miss, but strongly advising you against it, because it would be a debate or a petition you could never win. Ironically, if you had been fatally wounded or maimed you would have stood a chance, but not as things are. So, if you will take even more advice from me, let it be and I will see you are compensated. For I do believe in justice, and between you and me alone, I shall admit you were wronged, morally if not legally.'

He winked at her, and then looked ahead as they approached the end of the path. He placed her carefully back on her feet and pulled her to the side, behind the cover of trees for a moment.

Bethany was indeed nervous. His behaviour was confident like the gentry, as was his speech, yet he was peering through the tree cover as if not wanting to be seen by anyone. 'Sit for a while. They will not be long, then we shall enter and I shall see you well.'

'Who will not be long?' She squatted on her haunches next to him, not wanting to mess her dress up more than it had already been.

'Watch.' A carriage appeared from behind the large stone walls, leaving the manor house grounds between two large stone lions. It was followed a few minutes later by a cart filled with the house servants, which in turn was followed by two single lines of staff walking behind it in total silence, but the younger maids had a look of anticipation on their faces that was unmistakable; the same anticipation that Bethany herself had felt earlier in the day.

'Once they've turned the corner and are out of sight we shall enter,' he explained.

'We're not stealing anything; I'll not be a party to theft!' Bethany said, and stood up, ready to hobble the whole way back to Isadora.

'Steal!' He walked out on to the path. 'Miss, your honesty, considering your own situation in life, is both admirable and refreshing, and shall therefore be 'honestly' rewarded. Come with me to my home, and feel free to enter without embarrassment because the staff have been given permission to attend the fair and I have volunteered to watch over the house whilst they are away — at least until my mother and father return, for they will not endure the whole day. This is my home, miss. I do not steal either.'

He held out a hand and she took it as she walked, hobbled, her way to the courtyard, passing the two angry looking lions. She looked from one to the other, then saw the back of the manor house. Her mouth dropped open. It had a huge arch in the centre where the coach must have entered.

Behind was a building with a central bell tower whilst to either side of the courtyard were two long low buildings, one she could see was the laundry. Opposite was a blacksmiths, but the other rooms were behind a stone corridor so she could not determine their use.

'It's magnificent. Your home is beautiful,' she exclaimed and saw a broad grin break like sunshine across his face.

'Yes it is, but miss, this is the stable

yard. The manor house stands in front of it.'

Bethany stared at the ornate decoration on the building in front of her. 'This,' she pointed, 'is for the horses?'

'Yes,' he replied before leading her forwards.

'Lucky horses,' she muttered and was surprised when he gave her fingers a little squeeze, his eyes betraying a look of compassion rather than derision.

3

He took Bethany by the hand and led her into the building to the right, next to the abandoned blacksmiths and the wheelwrights. Bethany imagined this place as it would be normally, filled with activity, and a myriad of smells and sounds; people all doing their daily chores. Steam billowing out from the laundry, fire raging from the blacksmith's forge and hammers banging nails into boots on the anvils that were lined up before her in what was obviously the cobbler's room.

Richard walked straight to the back of the workroom; obviously fully aware of where things were kept. He rummaged around in the dark at the back under a work bench. She watched him as he stood up, returning to her with four polished black boots in his hands. 'Try these on for size,' he said, and pulled a stool over to her with his foot.

She felt the black leather with her finger before taking them off him. 'They're beautiful; the stitching is so even.' She looked up at him, his eyes were watching her curiously. 'It wouldn't be right . . . ' she said, swallowing back her desire to have them ' . . . I can't possibly take them off you.' She took a step back, her expression resolute but sombre.

'Whyever not?' He placed the stool square in front of her. 'Sit down and listen to me, Bethany. This gift is not a bribe, nor is it a ploy to win your . . . favours.' He paused as she stared at him, wide-eyed. The thought had never crossed her mind, until he mentioned it.

He smiled and continued, 'It is a gesture of apology — compensation for the frightening experience you had in the woods. This all belongs to me.' He waved one arm around him. Bethany did not know whether he meant the cobblers or the whole estate. But how could it if his father still lived?

She was left in little doubt as to what he referred when he concluded, 'This is not my parents', nor my brother's; the whole estate is mine, miss . . . ' He paused. 'What is your given name?' he asked her as if he had suddenly realised that he did not know what to call her; being found in the undergrowth doesn't give the opportunity for proper introductions.

She sat down upon the stool, aware of the state her attire was in. If Bethany had thought her hair was needing combing before Bill approached her and Kezzie on the moor, she dreaded to think what the mess looked like now.

Bill no longer seemed to be of any importance to her anymore. She had thought he was a fine man, but looking at this gentleman in front of her and the care he was taking of her, she realised just how naïve her view of Bill Judd had been.

He was selfish and uncaring, and he wanted to be with pretty Kezzie not

Bethany, and that had hurt.

'Bethany, sir,' she answered, and smiled at him.

'Well, 'Bethany Sir', you look much prettier when you smile, although you are already quite a striking young woman, if you'll excuse my being so bold. I would like you to understand that I cannot steal what is already mine, can I? So please accept the boots in the manner in which they are given.'

He sighed as her resolve did not change. 'They are intended to replace what was damaged in your fall. Next, we shall find something respectable for you to wear at the fair. That dress and shawl of yours are torn and tattered after your frightful experience in the woods . . . '

'Oh, no!' Bethany began to protest, 'they were already . . . ' she looked down a little shame-faced. Boldly, he cupped her chin in his hand tilting her head so that her eyes met his gaze. The skin of the palm of his hand was rough, as if it was used to a day's work, not what she had expected from a gentleman, not that she had been in such close contact with one before.

'If your outfit was once good enough to go to a fair, Miss Bethany, it certainly is not now, so, please, allow me to amend that, whilst you still have time to go and enjoy your day.' He removed his hand from her face and she stared at him for a moment, as each seemed lost in a private thought.

Bethany untied her old boots and busied herself trying on the new ones. The second pair she wore fitted her like a dream. Bethany hadn't even noticed that whilst she was preoccupied trying on the boots, and trying to hide the darns in her stockings, he had slipped out. She waited until he returned to show him the most polished and comfortable boots she had ever worn. They were new, not hand-me-downs or patched up, but new!

He arrived back with what looked like an arm full of mixed fabrics, as he neared she could see that in fact he carried a bundle of clothes.

'Come, you can use the laundry to wash and change in. No-one is around to see you, and I shall take myself elsewhere so that your privacy is assured. These are some of the garments that are kept here for our guests, in case they should stay over at short notice.'

Without giving her time to collect her thoughts she was marched over to the large laundry room. 'I have picked a fairly plain navy dress which will be serviceable, as well as becoming, matching the colour of your eyes.'

She could smell the strong aroma of starch and soap as she entered the large stone room. Stone sinks ran either side of a table strewn floor. It would be a warm and humid place to work, Bethany thought.

She picked up one of the large coarse brushes and stared at the large block of soap. She'd seen what the constant scrubbing could do to a girl's hands. Isadora had told her how she once worked in such a place and her hands were split open with sores and the like.

Wooden racks above her head were draped with white linen shirts, embroidered nightshifts and fine woollen stockings. He pulled a pair down and added them to her bundle of clothes.

'Wash and change and then come to the stable when you're ready and I shall take you to the fair. Hopefully, your day will improve from now on.' He smiled at her then left without saying a further word, but as she looked at the garments in her arms, she wondered how the day could improve from where she was now.

Bethany washed quickly. He had even left her a brush. She pulled on the white linen and lace under garments, then let the thick cotton dress slip over that. She had difficulty fastening all the hooks and eyes at the back of the bodice but managed. Then she sat down on a well worn wooden stool whilst she pulled on the warm woollen stockings, which had never once been darned.

With pride and a sense of joy she slipped on her new boots and laced them up with great care. Her hair was neatly fastened up and finally, her old bonnet replaced. She wrapped her old clothes up into a bundle and smoothed down her skirts. Dressed in her new navy dress she felt like a different person, confident.

She walked with her head held high, her shoulders back and a straight posture into the huge stable block.

Richard was patiently waiting for her next to a hitched up gig. As she entered he stared at her for a moment without speaking. Bethany thought for a moment that he had realised his error and was about to ask for everything back.

'You look . . . quite beautiful, Miss Bethany. Allow me.' He walked over to her and carefully removed her hat, replacing it with a straw bonnet that had a piece of navy velvet ribbon woven through it. Turning, he leaned into the gig and produced a wicker basket. From inside he pulled out a soft woollen shawl, the colour of sky blue. 'Here,' he handed it to her, 'wrap this around yourself and use the basket for your old clothes.'

'Mister . . . ?'

'Bartholomew,' he answered and held a hand out to guide her up into the gig.

'Mister Bartholomew, I don't know what to say to thank you enough for your generosity.' She stepped up into the gig, admiring the vehicle which had been polished and was grand in comparison to the back of a moors wagon.

Once seated beside her he felt, ever so lightly, the now dry graze where the bullet had just caught her. 'Bethany, God has protected you this morning and granted you a second chance at life. Make it better than it was before and tell your mama, that a gentleman accidentally knocked you down in the road and was so bereft that he had to do something in order to make amends.

'If you tell her the truth, I suspect you may be in for a remonstration for trespassing and entering the wood on your own. Regarding my brother's behaviour, it will not go unpunished. However, that is between myself and him. No-one would benefit from having your irate father coming here making threats or demands, so in this instance a white lie will, I am sure, be forgiven.'

She nodded her agreement. 'But sir, you are wrong.'

'Please, don't give me a sermon on the morality of telling untruths . . . '

'No, not that, I meant you were wrong to assume I have a mother and father, I don't.' She hugged the basket to her as he walked the horses out into the cobbled yard.

'Then, Miss Bethany, you are in greater need of that outfit than I had presumed.'

* * *

Kezzie was quite tired by the time they arrived at the fair, but was so excited and happy to be there that her joy alone kept her going — that and the presence of Bill Judd. He had his arm resting casually around her shoulders, occasionally squeezing her shoulder and winking at her. Bill was half holding and half leaning on her.

She wanted him to take some of his weight from her body, but did not speak out because she feared that if he did, he may remove it completely or be hurt, rejected.

Besides, she was all too aware that there were plenty of girls who would gladly have his attention, like bashful Bethany. She smiled at the thought that even the so practical and dull, plain Bethany had an eye for him. She looked up at the line of his jaw, roughly shaven, and smiled, as if she stood a chance with such a man.

'What yer lookin' at, Kez?' he asked, as he glanced at her, swinging the stick in his hand.

'You,' she answered and laughed.

'Admirin' what yer see?' His grin broadened.

'I was admiring how you handled young Bethany. I think she'd gone soft on you, Bill.'

'She's female, isn't she? What woman could resist?' He placed his lips on hers and stole a kiss. She protested, but not too strongly.

'Bill, stop your fooling around. People might see!' She pulled away slightly.

'Let them!' he said, but did not pursue the kiss.

'We have to take some care, Bill. My reputation will be ruined if you get too friendly like that!' Kezzie tried to sound firm.

'Yeah, since when have yer bothered about that, my little butterfly?'

Kezzie looked quite shocked. 'What do you mean by that, Bill?'

'I mean yer beautiful, now stop yer yakkin' before yer spoil the day.'

Kezzie wrapped an arm around his

waist and together they walked down the long road back into the vale. As they approached the gathering crowds, they separated, and he held his cane walking along with Flash by his side.

'Mornin' Bill,' an old farmer greeted him, and Bill touched the tip of his stick to his hat.

'Mornin' Jeb, have yer seen the competition then?' Bill asked and was instantly involved with a conversation. Kezzie stood to the side of him whilst the two ranted on about sheep, dogs, the moor, the gentry and the course.

Soon two more shepherds joined them. After what seemed like an age to the excited Kezzie, as she saw the players ready themselves for their show, dressed in colourful costumes and getting ready to perform. Bill turned to face her.

'Kez.' He tossed her a small coin, 'Run along and enjoy yerself, we have work to do.' He looked back to his group of friends.

Kezzie's cheeks flushed. 'But Bill, I

have something I wanted to tell you,' she said quietly, but loud enough for him to hear her. He glanced back and she fluttered her eyelashes at him, just a little, 'Privately.'

He leaned his face towards hers so that his mouth was near to her ear. She knew he could never resist her charms.

'Then save it for me until later, as now I have business to see to — so scatt!'

He placed an arm across one of his friend's shoulders and walked him and the other off to where they were selling jugs of ale. He didn't look back to see her ashen-struck face, but two of his friends did, and they both leered and grinned at her wickedly.

She turned on her heel and stormed off towards the players. If only she'd known he would desert her so easily, she thought to herself, she would never have allowed boring Bethany to return to the woman Isadora. At least Bethany would have stayed with her out of friendship, simple and reliable girl that she was.

Kezzie saw one of the players look her way, his eyes returning to settle their gaze on her as she pushed to the front of the crowd. He winked at her and she smiled sweetly back at the painted face, letting her curls bounce a little as she did so. He blew her a discreet kiss, her cheeks flushed just a little, but her eyes met his and as the people around her giggled at the actor's impish behaviour, they both knew their time would come.

Suddenly, the fair had more interest to her than Bill Judd. So Kezzie decided whilst he played with the sheep she'd find her own entertainment, and relaxed as she watched the performance begin.

* * *

The gig bumped its way along the road. For all he was insistent that she still went to the fair and enjoyed her day, he did not seem to be travelling at a swift pace. In fact he had the horse doing more of an even plod. They rode past the walled garden and rounded the front of the large house with its many chimney stacks reaching up into the sky.

All Bethany could do was stare in wonder at the ornate frontage. Tall columns of stone pillars framed the large black doors. Bethany looked on in awe as the horse pulled them onwards and started down the long drive. More statues of lions lined the long drive, which was already lined with young trees. Sheep strolled freely about eating the already short grass.

'Your home is beautiful, sir. When the dowager lived here it was said to be much neglected and very grim, but this is magnificent.' She meant every word of it because she could see that he had a vision for the place.

Bethany pictured the trees full grown, offered a wind-break from the gales that could sweep along the open vale. This would offer shelter to visitors, but more than that, it would give the home a focus instead of staring at an open expanse of land, and a narrow drive facing a dense wooded slope leading to the moor.

'It was indeed run down when I first saw it, but after months of hard work it is almost as I wish it to be, at least on the outside. There are still many rooms inside which need attention, but the house is now functioning as a respectable home, fit for my parents in their latter years. With the workshops staffed and working they are paying towards the renovation which still needs to be done. One day I hope to . . . ' He stopped talking for a moment and looked at her. 'I did not wish to bore you with the detail. We shall progress to the fair.'

'Indeed, you have not! I find your passion for it charming.' Bethany was surprised when, having heard her reply, he stopped the gig.

'Miss Bethany, do you really mean that, or are you merely being polite?'

Bethany wondered why he should

doubt her words, but she answered him honestly. 'I really mean it. You talk about it as though you have worked tirelessly to bring it to this point and I think that is a huge achievement. You have seen how to make it live again, and planned for a future. No, I think you will make this old house an estate to be proud of. What's more you have given people in desperate need of a wage, hope for once.'

'Hold tightly,' he said in response, and turned the gig around in a sweeping circle, towards the front steps of the hall. Jumping down he came around to Bethany's side of the vehicle and offered her his hand.

'Miss, I promise to take you at speed to the town before noon, but first allow me to give you a quick tour of my home . . . and my vision.' He smiled with genuine warmth that both pleased and thrilled her.

She took his hand and stepped down next to him leaving the basket with her old attire in the gig. He still had a hold of her hand as he led her up the stone steps and into the house through the large doors.

The sight that greeted her inside stunned her. The newly painted hallway opened out into a hexagon shape. There were two doors to the left and a further two to the right, the main staircase lying straight ahead of them; this again split to the left and right on the first landing.

She walked into the centre of the tiled floor and let her sight travel toward the dome above. It was made of glass. Filtered sunlight spilled down, bouncing from the pale lemon walls to the polished floor, highlighting the features of the people that looked down upon her from the large portraits that adorned the walls. She turned slowly, in a full circle, taking in all the detail of polished oak and ornate plastework alike, until her eyes rested upon Richard's face as he stood, silently watching her.

'It's truly delightful. Did you design

this? I can't believe the dowager ever saw her home so bright.' She raised her arms as she spoke to emphasise the splendour of it, yet at the same time it was simple in design. He had cleverly used natural light to give the place a sense of space. Even on a dull day, there would be no gloom here.

'Yes, I did, but nobody who has seen it, has appreciated it like I do.' He looked away quickly. 'Until you entered,' he said softly. Then, as if shaking himself out of his thoughts he suddenly strode forward. 'Come, I shall show you quickly what is still to be done.' He took hold of her hand and started to almost run up the stairs with her. Swept along with his enthusiasm Bethany was on the third step before she even realised what she was doing.

He stopped with her and looked almost disappointed. 'I'm sorry, but I don't think I should . . . I mean . . . '

'You mean that I am man and you are woman!' His voice was quite abrupt, but he sat down on a step two up from her, letting her hand fall to her side. 'Look, I could have . . . done anything to you when you were in the woods or changing in the laundry, couldn't I?'

Bethany looked at him and crossed her arms in front of her as she would when one of Isadora's boys started setting lip to her.

He seemed humoured by her change of attitude, and folded his arms also. 'You want to see the challenges I still have to face, don't you? Bethany, to hell with what people would say! I assure you we are quite alone. Come, I shall not do anything other than ask your opinion, of that I can give you my word.'

He turned and started climbing the stairs once more.

'You'd ask my opinion, why?' she asked.

'Because you understand my vision. I can see it in your eyes. But I'm exhausted by what I have done so far, and I need to be inspired. So my little inspiration, humour me, whilst we still have time to get you to the fair.' He did not wait for her reply, but continued up the stairs.

By the time he had reached the landing she was by his side. No one had wanted her opinion before, and as she was dressed as a lady, she had to admit she felt truly inspired.

4

A blast of cold air swept up the stairs as the main doors flew open. Richard looked anxiously at Bethany, stepping slightly in front of her, until he could see clearly who had followed them inside.

'My dear brother . . . ' Bartholomew's voice boomed out from the entrance hall. 'What do we have here — a bird in your nest?' No wonder you did not want to come to the fair with Mama and Papa.'

His brother stood facing the stairs, a twisted smile on his face as he casually folded his arms and looked up at Richard who glanced down at Bethany's embarrassed face.

He winked at her discreetly, before standing square to face his brother. Bethany suspected that he was slightly shaken by the change of events, and did not like being caught unawares.

'Don't be absurd and vulgar! You insult my guest with your comments, Bartholomew. Why are you returned so early are Mother and Father here also?'

Richard spoke calmly as if Bartholomew was holding him up and was no more than an annoyance with his interruption.

'No, you need not worry, they are still pre-occupied with the local dross. You have no idea the state of some of them. No, I forgot something and had to return. So are you going to introduce me to your *guest*, or not. Where are your manners, Richard?'

He placed one foot on the first stair.

'I am Miss Bethany Young,' she answered, covering a slight hesitation from Richard as he did not know her surname.

'Well, Miss Bethany Young, what is a beautiful flower such as you, doing on the upper landing of our home with a weed such as my dear younger brother?' He walked up the stairs until he was level with them. 'Your reputation, miss . . .'

' . . . Is in no danger of being tarnished at all, of that you can be quite assured. I was showing Miss Young around the house. Now you had better collect what you had forgotten and return to my parents, who will be waiting for you. As the fair is in your honour you can hardly absent yourself.' Richard stared defiantly at his taller brother, who obviously enjoyed Richard's discomfort.

'Tell me, miss, why were you about here?' Bartholomew ignored Richard completely.

'She was about to decide whether or not she would be interested in a position as companion to Mother. You know how much she needs somebody reliable to help her,' Richard said quickly.

'Do you have good references, miss?' Bartholomew asked with an almost teasing air about his question.

'I have seen her references, Bartholomew.'

'I'm sure you have!' he replied.

'Do not concern yourself. I would

hardly allow someone of an unsuitable nature to keep company with our mother, would I?' Richard looked at his brother sternly.

'No, Richard, you would always do what was correct, of that I have no doubt.' He looked at Bethany and winked. 'Why do you think he has so many lions out there?' He leaned towards her and whispered into her ear, 'Thinks he's Richard the Lionheart.'

Richard ignored his brother's tease and continued, 'We have to face the fact that Mama is quite fragile now, but this lady will need to see the house first so that she can understand that at present it is a home that is not quite all it would appear from its frontage.

'So I want this done before Mama returns from her outing. I shall speak to her about it once the detail is sorted out, which is why I have been keeping my actions to myself, as finding the right person for her is essential. So be about *your* business, sir, and we shall join you all very soon.'

Richard took two steps up the next flight of richly carpeted stairs and turned around to face Bethany who was looking quite stunned by events.

'Miss, if you follow me, I shall show you what is intended to be the companion's rooms, when they are finished being decorated, that is.' He held an arm out to show her the way he intended her to go.

Bethany stepped past Bartholomew. 'Excuse me, sir. It has been a pleasure to meet you,' she said politely smiling up at him, trying to keep up with Richard's swift thoughts and actions, and then she followed Richard.

'The pleasure has been . . . all mine,' Bartholomew said loudly and swooped low in an exaggerated bow. 'I assure you, miss. Until we meet again, Miss Bethany, I shall look forward to our reunion.'

She glanced back to see him almost running back down the stairs. Richard had wandered down a corridor and into one of the rooms. Bethany eagerly followed him. This world she had entered was so far removed from her cottage. In fact the cottage could have fitted into the entrance hall alone.

She was so glad she had washed and combed out her hair the evening before, in preparation for the fair. She wondered if she ever would see the jugglers, players or Bill win or lose in his competition. Did she even care?

No, she had found out what it was like to be inside the world of the gentry; high ceilings, magnificent paintings and carpets of rich colours and quality wool. Everywhere was a feast of beautiful, ornate delights. Any one of them she could have stood and wondered at.

After a few moments, she heard the large door close in the hall below. Entering the room, Bethany saw Richard staring out of a large window that overlooked the drive. He ran a hand through his short dark brown hair as he stood watching Bartholomew ride away across the open grass at full gallop.

'He still thinks he is leading the

charge in the field of war!' Richard said contemplatively and shook his head. 'Oh dear, what have I done, Miss Bethany?' he spoke softly.

'Lied, in a very plausible way and in the process saved my reputation, I hope,' she answered honestly.

He looked at her and a slight smile crossed his lips. 'Perhaps not. Can you read?'

'You mean my reputation lies in ruins?' she exclaimed.

'No, that is safe, on that I have already given you my word. No, I referred to the lie. Can you read?' he repeated his question.

'James taught me how to read the Bible, so yes. I used to read it out to him at night. It was his most treasured possession. He tried to teach Amos, Ezra and Zach but they were more interested in being outdoors working on the land.' She saw his eyes widen a little as if he was inspired once more.

'Bethany, are you free?' he asked excitedly.

‘In what way, sir?’ she answered, not quite following his meaning.

‘Are you free to work here — if you so wished to? Do you have a man? You said that you were an orphan, but do you have a family of your own?’ he looked almost excited at the prospect of whatever he was planning.

‘Well, no, not like you mean. I live with Isadora and James, who work at the poor-house. They have three sons and I help Isadora to look after them. In return I have space for my bed and I receive my keep. In a way they have been like my adoptive parents, but they are not really — they do care for me, though. They are very nice people, but I’m not *family* in any sense of the words, sir.’

He took her hand in his. ‘Then you are free to work here as a personal companion and maid to my mother — for a decent wage?’ He looked at her almost anxious that she replied in the affirmative.

‘But . . . ’

‘No *buts* allowed.’

‘My education is limited,’ she persisted, ‘and I don’t know the ways of a lady, or how they behave, or how to live in a house such as this . . . ’

Bethany’s head was filled with questions and thoughts of the sudden turn of events and her good fortune. Yes, she wanted to, but surely his mother would ridicule her, but then as she glanced down she saw the dress, and realised that even his brother had not. It was the situation he had found them in — a man and woman alone in a house climbing the stairs together — he had mocked that, catching, as he thought, his brother up to no good, not her, or her attire. Bethany had been dressed respectably and had been treated in the same manner by a war hero.

‘Admit it, Beth, you would like to say yes, wouldn’t you?’ he said; his arms folded as he casually leaned against the wall. ‘Say yes and I’ll teach you all you would need to know, then you can inspire me with your fresh vision as I finished the house.'

'I don't know what Isadora would say. Or James for that matter.'

He stood straight. 'Then we shall waste no more time. You will have plenty of opportunity to see the house when you move in. I shall take you back to your Isadora. You can collect your things from there and I shall make all well with them. You shall meet my dear mama and your new life here shall begin. Don't worry about Bartholomew. He becomes easily bored; he won't stay around here for long. Soon London's lure will call him back and we shall have peace once more.'

Before long they were back in the gig. This time he flicked the reins and the vehicle travelled at a pace that was swift. She held on to the seat with one hand and her hat with the other enjoying the thrill of the ride as her adventure continued.

'We'll sweep around by the fair, but shall not stop until we have sorted out our business with your family.' He looked at her. 'You are not disappointed at missing most of the fair are you? Were you meeting friends there?'

'No, I'm not disappointed at all. I'm having an entertaining day anyway,' she almost shouted her words so that he could hear her over the noise of the horse's hooves.

He laughed as they approached the village. 'So what were you doing on your own in our woods, anyway?' he asked and looked at her.

'You have only just thought to ask me!' She laughed at him, and he slowed down the pace of the vehicle as they approached the village. She let go of her bonnet and sobered herself before answering simply, 'Why, going to the fair, of course!'

They slowed almost to a stop as they picked their way slowly through the busy market square. The horse's hooves clattered against the cobbled stones competing with the noise of players, a fiddler, bidding shouts from the auction pen and the general hubbub of an excited crowd. Stalls hastily set up sold everything from bread to wool, cloth to ale.

'My parents must be at the inn with my brother away from the merry throng and banter,' Richard said, as he saw the carriage and driver waiting patiently at the side.

'Listen to that!' Bethany exclaimed, as a woman with a large chest and a painted face was bellowing out a song from a makeshift stage. 'It sounds like a sick cow!' she said, and chuckled to herself.

'That is supposed to be opera, Beth. It is the music of the rich people in London. However, sung like that it is barely recognisable. But she is enjoying her moment, and at least she is having some fun.' He smiled warmly at her. 'She is entertaining others, too.' He pointed to a group of people holding their ears and laughing merrily at her.

Bethany was still smiling when she saw the back of Kezzie, going into an alleyway beside one of the makeshift tents. ‘Oh, Mister . . . Richard, could we stop for just a moment so that I can tell a friend of my intentions . . . she may look for me,’ she added the last statement weakly as her heart might wish it so, but her head told her that she was far from Kezzie’s mind.

Richard found a place to stop the gig where it would be safe for a few moments. To her surprise he stepped down also.

‘I should not wish to lose you in the crowd, Bethany. Your day started ominously enough with you wandering around by yourself. I shall be glad to meet your friend or wait discreetly somewhere, whilst you share your news with her, then we shall have to be on our way unless seeing the festivities has caused you to have a change of mind?’ He looked quite serious and waited for her reply.

‘Oh no, I haven’t, nothing of the kind! No, it is just that I saw my friend, Kezzie, she went down here.’ Bethany started to walk towards the alley. Richard said nothing but followed a couple of paces behind her.

The narrow snicket led on to a small yard behind some old cottages. At first there seemed to be no-one about, the noise and excitement of the fair was almost dulled by the buildings. Opposite them, was a low tiled building with the door left slightly ajar. It appeared to be a saddler's workroom.

Bethany walked over to the door as she heard Kezzie's unmistakable giggle. Precariously, she slowly pushed the door slightly open. In the dusky light she could not see movement within, but she could hear muffled voices or sounds.

Bethany felt very nervous, unsure she should be there at all. She was about to call out her friend's name; her eyes were looking around the small room and not downwards to the floor.

Her mouth opened to speak out, but it was Richard's hand that cupped it and his finger pointed downwards.

From under the large bench at the back of the work room they could see four booted feet.

This made Bethany step back into the yard, almost trampling Richard in her path. She looked at him, lost for words, and then stared at the cobbled stone.

Something colourful caught her eye and she bent down, picking up the pale blue ribbon that had adorned her friend's hat. There was no doubt who it was that had literally sunk so low. She wrapped the piece of ribbon around her fingers and almost ran back in a hurry to the gig.

Bethany was enraged by the girl's behaviour. To think she had sought to go to the fair in the company of a girl with such loose morals! But more than that, Richard had seen her also.

Bethany found the whole experience totally humiliating. What if he presumed her to be like her friend? She would hardly be fitting company for his mother.

She climbed back up, ignoring the joviality surrounding her and fixing her eyes on the horse's back as Richard took up the reins and moved the vehicle onwards.

What could she say to him? There was no mistaking what had been happening.

The little fool, was that what it took to catch the like of Bill Judd?

She hugged herself tightly holding the shawl around her as they came to the far side of the village. She was glad to be leaving the fair. For months it had meant so much to her, but now she wished it far enough.

Sheepdogs barked excitedly ahead of them. She recognised one as Flash, Bill's dog, running alongside their horse and for a moment thought that it must be looking for its master. Suddenly, the dog ran in front of the horse causing Richard to swerve dramatically. Fortunately, he was a skilled driver and no harm was done to the dog, horse, passengers or the gig.

'Flash!' followed by a whistle called the dog to order as Bill Judd ran over from where he had been talking to a group of friends. He looked at Richard and doffed his cap, 'Sorry, sir. Beggin' yer pardon, but I'd just won the competition and forget meself in the moment of celebration. It won't happen again. Pardon to you, miss, too . . . ' his eyes fixed on Bethany's face, who was already staring at Bill as if she'd seen a ghost.

'No harm done, Bill,' she said sweetly, and watched as the stunned figure stepped back to let the gig pass. He was speechless. From the dismissed girl with the soleless shoe she had transformed into a lady sitting upon a gig with a gentleman by her side. The victory of the moment was not lost on her, but one question resounded in her head: If Bill is here, then who was Kezzie with?

An empty feeling filled her as she realised the things Isadora had said about the girl were true, and she had been an utter fool not to see it. As they climbed form the vale to the open moor road away from the village she looked at Richard.

'I . . . I am so sorry. If you wish to withdraw your offer I shall understand.'

'You don't have to say a word. If you had had any notion what the girl was like you would not have led me in there as if we were to join her for tea. The shame is all hers and none of it yours, Bethany. Somehow, you just don't belong with them.' He looked at her and she could not help herself grin as he was laughing openly.

'She's no friend of mine, not now. Let us say no more about it, especially in front of Isadora and James . . . please?' Bethany stopped laughing.

'My lips are sealed,' he answered before adding, 'Somehow, I think life with Miss Bethany in my home will never be dull. You have a knack of making the ordinary a little extra.'

Bill strode into the village searching for Kezzie. What had been happening whilst he had been winning his competition and why wasn't she there to celebrate with him? The selfish little trollop! Well, he was certainly going to celebrate when he got his hands on her. She was just like Flash, eager to please her master and Bill knew she was his through and through.

But where was she? And why was that wench, Bethany, sitting on a gig dressed like the toffs? Perhaps he'd read her wrong. Still, if she had a hankering for him he may be able to make her see the error of his ways. One for each hand, he mused to himself.

Bill beamed broadly as he pushed through the crowds. There in the distance he saw her. She was fiddling with her bonnet, and looking around her on the floor. Bill stepped in front of her, lifted her head up with his hand and slapped a passionate kiss firmly on her lips. She almost squealed and shook uncontrollably. He loved the effect he had on women. When he let her loose he saw her cheeks were flushed red.

'Why, Kezzie, you're keen today. Come let's find a quiet spot.' He glanced down the alleyway she was standing next to.

'Bill, I've lost Mama's ribbon, she'll give me hell!' Kezzie was looking all over the ground as he led her back down the alley to the square behind.

'Then think about me. It will make yer heart sing.'

Kezzie's head shot up as he pushed the door open of the saddler. He pulled her in by the hand. 'Here'll do.' He spun her around and rested her on the work bench pushing the tools to the side.

'Bill, what do you think your doing? Anyone could come in!'

'Come on, lass.' He pulled her to his body kissing her mouth eagerly.

Kezzie pulled her head away. 'Bill, I love you. You know I do, but I've been trying to tell you all week, but you won't listen to me — Bill, I'm having your baby!'

Bill stopped fumbling and looked at

her. ‘Yer not tryin’ to trick Bill, are yer?’

‘No, Bill, I’d never do that to yer, yer know that.’ She looked at him through watery eyes.

‘Then there’s no reason to say no anymore.’ He pulled her close again. ‘I’ll save yer reputation and take yer for me wife.’

5

Kezzie watched as he strode meaningfully off, whistling loudly, to tell his friends he was about to wed. He had taken it all within his stride, almost as if it was expected.

'Sort yerself out, woman, and then join me at the ale hut. I'll break our news and we shall all celebrate together. Mam will be real glad to hear that I'm settlin' down with a pretty girl.' He looked at her thoughtfully. 'She likes bairns and could do with an extra pair of hands around the farm. Besides, you'll be there whenever I need yer, without that mother of yours lookin' down her nose at me and Flash.'

He paused and winked, then hesitated, his mood, his manner changed as he walked back over to her. Kezzie knew that look. It came over him just before he was about to do something, normally something bad.

She smiled at him as he neared trying to force the tears back that were threatening to escape her lids, so that she looked every inch a happy young woman who had just been proposed to, for that was the most romantic proposal she would receive from Bill Judd.

She was surprised that she found it difficult to pretend. He placed a hand on each of her shoulders and rubbed them gently. Kezzie tried not to tremble.

'Kezzie, you wouldn't be playin' Bill for a fool now, would you? This baby, it will look like Bill now, won't it?' His grip tightened and both his thumbs found the front of her throat. She swallowed.

'No-one could play you for a fool, Bill. No-one.' She looked at him. with her eyes wide open and as honest as she could make them.

'Good, because no-one who has, is still walkin' straight, Kez.' He kissed her lips tenderly and left her to her thoughts, troubled as they were.

Kezzie stood there and breathed heavily. The tears trickled down her cheeks, for after being besotted by the man for over a year she now hated him. She had discovered something that very afternoon, something precious and too late; Kezzie now knew what a man's touch could feel like, the player had been gentle and fun, Kezzie had learned and she cursed her own stupidity.

Now, she was stuck with a baby, a bully, and destined to work until her hair had lost its natural bounce and her hands were as hard as Isadora's. She sunk to her knees and sobbed into her hands, knowing this was not the future her mama had planned for her.

* * *

'My village is down there.' Bethany pointed as the road ahead branched off to the right. 'It's a steep road that descends through a forest, and sweeps by the village pond and church. It is not very big and the homes are small, but the people are friendly — usually.' Bethany was quite excited. 'The poor-house, where Isadora works, is at the other end of town. It looks bleak from the outside, but she tries to make things as pleasant for them as she is allowed to. You'll like her, I'm sure. Oh look, there she is now!' Bethany was almost trying to stand to catch Isadora's attention.

Isadora had obviously seen the lady in the gig waving to her. She approached apprehensively and it was only when she was standing a few feet away, that they saw the realisation dawn on her face that it was her Bethany dressed so fine.

Bethany smiled from ear to ear at the shock showing on the older woman's face.

'What is this?' Isadora's eyes were looking from Bethany to Richard and back. Questions were obviously filling her head, but she hurried over to greet Bethany who had eagerly climbed down from the gig. 'What ever has happened to you, girl? Where are your own clothes and why are you in such a fine vehicle with such a fi . . . gentleman? What has become of Kezzie? Did you desert her? Has there been an accident?'

'It's all right, Isadora.' Bethany tried not to think about what had happened to Kezzie. 'I've been offered a position up at the old dowager's house. It's splendid and Mister Richard wants me to be a companion to his mama, and he owns it now of course, not the dowager and . . . '

'And, I think I need a cup of tea. Please come in, sir. I think you need to explain the nonsense that is pouring out of my Bethany's mouth.' She opened the door to the cottage and led them inside. The table was as always set fresh with a linen cloth placed over it.

James loved to come home to a clear table with the square of linen on top of it. It was what he called civilised. Of course no-one was allowed to eat on it; it was there purely to dress the empty table.

Richard had to bend low under the beam and was soon seated in the chair by the fire grate. Isadora rescued the dying fire embers.

'Sir, I implore you to tell me honestly what has happened to my girl and why is she not wearing her own clothes?' Isadora looked at him quite sternly.

'Isad . . . ' Bethany began.

'You be quiet, and let the gentleman explain himself. This is your reputation that is at stake here, girl. You come back to me, on yer own, dressed like that in a gent's vehicle, what on earth will folk be thinking?' She placed a firm fist on each hip and looked at Richard, straight in the eye.

'I can't speak for others, ma'am, but I can tell you that after Miss Bethany was involved in a small accident after falling into some undergrowth, I offered her help and discovered an intelligent young woman who, I believe, would make an excellent companion for my mother.' Richard's manner was both polite and relaxed. Isadora was listening to his every word.

'Where was Kezzie when you stumbled?' she asked Bethany directly.

'My sole had come off my old boot at the toe, and I was on my way back here when I stumbled.' Bethany was more bothered about covering over what had happened in the woods than protecting the reputation of her fallen and two-faced friend.

'So you left the girl out on the moor on her own?' Isadora queried. 'This does not sound like something you would do, Bethany.' Isadora returned her attention to Richard.

'No, not at all, I wouldn't have done that to her.' She glanced at Richard knowing that Kezzie had not hesitated to abandon her. 'Kezzie went on to the fair with Bill Judd and his dog.'

'That figures, so she left you to walk back on yer own. She would have stuck like glue to you if she'd known you were about to be rescued by a gentleman such as this.' Without waiting for further comment she spoke to Richard, 'So, what are you proposing, sir?'

'If you will allow it, I shall take Bethany back home to be formally introduced to my mother, and providing that all is well between them I would like her to move into the rooms next to Mother's when the refurbishment is completed.

'I should estimate it will take two more weeks, until then I will see she has a suitable room made available. I would like to offer her a fair remuneration and a one off payment to yourself so that you are able to find an extra pair of hands to help here, if needed.'

Bethany looked at her with great excitement in her eyes. Isadora's face could not hide the sadness she felt, though. 'Lass, whenever will I see you again?' Isadora asked, for it was the separation that obviously concerned her greatly.

Richard laughed, then excused himself. 'I can assure you I neither wish to imprison your . . . daughter or my mother. Mother is most keen to develop her charitable work and has her sights set on the poorhouse. She will no doubt be visiting there soon enough. I will arrange for you to visit each other every alternate Sunday. Now, is this suitable to you, for I have to return shortly and . . . '

A large figure filled the doorway. 'You are talking to the wrong person. Mother, I was informed my girl has been travellin' around the countryside un-chaperoned with a man. 'Tis talk like that, that starts rot!' James walked in and Richard stood to greet him.

Far from being daunted he looked relaxed and smiled broadly at him. 'James, I hadn't realised that it was you Bethany was referring to. No wonder she has a gentle manner and a sound education.' James swung his arms around Richard and the two hugged each other for a moment.

'Will you allow her to come back with me?' Richard said.

'Aye, go and pack yer things, lass. Young Dick will see you all right, but you make sure she is, my man, or friendship will go out of the window. That girl is a good 'un, I don't want her spoilin'.' James' manner surprised Isadora and Bethany.

'Woman, I pulled this boy out from a bog by his neck when he visited his aunt, the old dowager, many a year ago. She would've tanned his hide raw if she'd known. He was always gettin' into scrapes, but yer did well for yerself. Sorry, you were injured so bad by the Frenchies, but like everything else, yer pulled through!' James sat down as Richard blushed slightly at the reference. 'Tea woman, they can't go back without sharin' our victuals first!'

Isadora set to removing the linen, but James stopped her. We eat like civilised folk.' He nodded and Bethany ran up her rickety ladder to collect her few things whilst Isadora cut the bread and cheese.

Bethany could not help thinking about how excited she was when she arose that very morning contemplating the fair, but with no knowledge that the day would turn out to be even more exciting than that.

They were all seated at the table enjoying the tea and conversation when the door was flung open wide. 'Where's my girl? What have you done with my Kezzie?'

'Why Sarah, whatever has come over you?' Isadora stood as Sarah Farmer entered her cottage uninvited. The woman was slender and was neatly dressed. Always 'a cut above' was how Isadora described her to Bethany. They never saw eye to eye on anything. Isadora was down to earth and Sarah was always looking beyond herself.

'Dear sir, excuse my bursting in on your private party like this, but I'm racked with worry.' She looked at Richard, but it was James who spoke.

' 'Tis all right, lass, your Kezzie is being looked after, I'm informed.'

'I wasn't talking to you, Jim Updale. I was addressing this young gentleman here.' She looked at Bethany, in her new clothes. 'My girl, how you've changed from your usual ragged attire. What have you done with my Kezzie?'

'She was with Bill Judd the last time I saw her, as she walked off with him leaving me on my own.' Bethany had not meant to be so forthright, but she was annoyed with the woman for interrupting what had been a pleasant half hour and her last chance to sit down with Isadora and James before starting her new life.

'Wash your mouth out, girl! My Kezzie is a lady! She doesn't go gallivanting around the countryside with young men!' She turned to Richard. 'Sir, if you would be so kind as to give me a lift back to the fair on your return I could find my poor lost girl and see her back safely myself.'

She looked at Richard with the most charmingly pathetic expression, that Bethany had ever seen her use.

Richard stood up, 'We can drop you as we go, then she can explain herself how she came to desert Miss Updale here, on the moor road.'

'Miss Updale?' Sarah repeated. 'Oh, you mean Bethany!' she said in a surprised tone.

'You . . . ' Bethany stepped forward and stopped Isadora from launching into a verbal attack against the woman, whilst James looked on amused.

'It's all right, Ma,' Bethany deliberately gave Isadora the rarely used title. 'Richard knows that I am not actually family, he understands.' Isadora took the hint and hugged her instead.

'You take care of my girl, you hear!' Isadora said as Richard climbed up into the gig. It was a bit of a squash but all three managed.

'You have my word,' he said and smiled at James.

'That's good enough for me, Richard.' James' voice boomed across them. Sarah was taking all in as they rode off, her leg resting against Richard's as they trotted along the road.

'This is very kind of you, sir,' she whispered.

'I know,' he replied and winked at Bethany. The three fell into an awkward silence, and Bethany wished they would soon be at the fair, if only to be rid of Sarah and have Richard's company all to herself once more; for she liked it very much.

6

Bethany squashed up at one side and Sarah at the other. The woman was 'all bone' as Isadora described her, so she didn't take up much room. It was really hard for Bethany to wave goodbye to a tearful Isadora, but Richard had promised that she would be seeing her and his word was good enough for her.

'How did you come to lose your clothes, Bethany?' Sarah asked in what was a deceptively innocent sounding tone.

'She didn't,' Richard replied not taking his eyes from the road. He quickened the pace and the two women both clung to the side of the seat. 'She is wearing her own clothes.' He offered no more explanation and Bethany made no attempt to converse with Sarah.

It did not take long for them to reach the descent to the vale and the fair.

They had to pull over and wait whilst a caravan of three covered wagons with brightly dressed players pulled their burden up the steep bank.

Sarah instantly squealed with delight. 'Oh, isn't it gay! You must allow me to treat you for your kindness, sir!' Sarah exclaimed. 'What a shame that I did not come with the girls, then all manner of inconvenience could have been avoided.' She glared at Bethany who merely looked the other way.

She stared at the last wagon, a hand had pulled back the canvas slightly, and the interior looked warm and sumptuous with warm coloured fabrics draped inside. She thought she heard a woman gasp, but then realised it would be no more than a trick of the wind that was stirring.

As soon as the vehicles were safely past them Richard carried on. Almost as an afterthought he answered Sarah, 'No, that will not be necessary. We have to press on.'

He stopped the gig by the edge of the

town and helped Sarah down. 'I hope you shall find your daughter and her friend well enough.' Without waiting for a reply he took his seat in rather more comfort and moved the vehicle off.

'That lady has the nerve of the devil,' he said quietly, 'pardon me for saying so.'

'You are pardoned, sir, for Isadora has made far more direct and accurate observations over the years. They are as chalk and cheese!'

Kezzie was still in a huddle when she heard the sound of footsteps approaching over the cobblestones. She rubbed her eyes to see who it was. Expecting it to be Bill, angry with her for not joining him already, she was very surprised when a hand gently stroked her arm.

'Hey, little missy, you all right?' the voice, although deep was equally gentle as the touch. She knew who it was straight away.

'Oh, Adam!' She looked into the player's deep blue eyes and fell into his arms. He swept her up as if she weighed no more than a feather and carried her out of the yard by the snicket at the back, away from the fair and the crowd.

Before she lifted her head away from his chest, she was already being placed down on a bed within a covered wagon. It was only narrow and was made of wool sacks, packed with soft wadding.

'Tell Adam, what makes you, so lively a young woman, turn so sad? I thought we had fun earlier. Do you now regret your passion, miss?' He smiled impishly then winked at her.

'Oh, Adam, we did, and I was so happy, but what can you be thinking of me.' She placed her hand over her mouth. 'My fiancé, he . . . he is not like you.' She looked down; the misery she felt coupled with the physical exhaustion threatened to overwhelm her.

'Hey, if he doesn't treat you right, then you don't go out with him. If he is a big brute then he shall crush this little flower to pieces and all your petals will wilt.'

As he spoke his hands did motions to

illustrate the flower falling sadly to the ground. Instantly, she smiled at him. She felt like a child, and he a jester to make her happy, just to please her alone.

'Adam, you make all that is black sound white. It is not as simple as that. I have to marry him, because . . . '

'No, you don't! You can be free, little one.' He was smiling at her as he offered her a goblet half filled with wine. 'We have to leave here now before the night closes in.'

'I do, but you don't understand.' She sipped the liquid and looked at him amazed. 'You live like a gypsy yet drink from a cup that would serve a lord!' She sipped some more feeling the warmth of the drink drift down through her veins.

'Yes, I do understand, little one. Your belly has a fullness to it. It has a life of its own, does it not?' He looked at her and she stared at him.

'You knew? Then why did you come and find me, Adam?' her eyes had filled with warm tears again.

'Because I heard your man bragging to his friends that he had landed himself the young filly in the village and he'd soon have yer 'whipped into shape'. Pardon my interrupting in your affairs, but I didn't think the little flower that had hugged Adam so tightly would take to being whipped, besides, I like the shape you're already in.' He placed a hand on her stomach lightly. 'You need to take care.'

'How can I? I carry his child! Adam, I will be the joke of the village. My mama will skin me if I don't marry him, but when she finds it's to one of the Judds I'll never be able to visit her again. She wanted better than that for me, Adam. I've let everyone down and I'd hate to live on a farm. I'm scared, but I can't run . . . I'm trapped.'

She started to cry, but the vehicle started to move forwards. 'Where are we going?' she asked him nervously as it tilted to climb the steep bank up to the moor road.

'You can leave here now and return to your drunkard of a man or, my little flower, you can come with Adam and follow the road; see where it goes and discover who you will meet along the way. I cannot promise our paths will ever turn back this way but it shall never end, young missy, for Adam travels along life's journey with nothing but expectation that every day will be different.'

He held her trembling hand, 'Come with me, with my group of players. We do not go hungry, we carry no past and each new day we create our own future. You are a soul who will always want more. You shall make a natural actress; you have the character and the looks, come and find your future with us . . . and don't look back!'

He lifted the flap at the back of the wagon and the fair's lights still shone in the distance. They passed a gig that had pulled to the side of the road, to move out of their way. She heard her mother's shrill tone and saw her hat. A young woman turned as she let out a gasp.

'Bethany!' Whatever had been happening whilst she had been . . . at the fair? She had no idea, but if it involved her mother being called for and a gentleman in a gig, it looked to her like she was in for even more trouble than even she had realised.

She smiled warmly at Adam, brushed her tears away with her hands and said quietly, 'Take me into the unknown, Adam. I have no life to have worth living here.'

He let the canvas fall back down and hugged her.

'You shall be a free sprit and your baby will grow into the best of actors!' He hugged her and she felt his warmth against her as she melted into his arms. Kezzie swallowed and promised herself she would make this work, she would be free.

7

'Richard! Richard! Where have you been? We've been looking everywhere for you. We thought you'd been kidnapped by those French, as if they'd come to get revenge for what dear Bartholomew did to Napoleon.'

A fragile looking old lady came rushing across the hallway from the morning room as Richard entered. Bartholomew was leaning casually against the door frame not at all flustered, Bethany thought to herself, despite the woman's obvious distress.

'I'm fine, Mama. In fact, I have a pleasant surprise for you.' He gave the lady a warm smile. She positively flounced with lace, from her cap to her shawl to the kerchief she carried in her hand. Against her grey-white silky hair she almost had an ethereal air to her which did not seem to belong to the reality of the world.

Richard gently released her grip and instead held her hand in his. Like leading a lost child, he walked her over and Bethany could see the affection he held for this fragile lady.

'This, Mama, is Miss Bethany Updale. She is here to keep you company and stop you fretting so when you find yourself on your own for a few moments. You have a marvellous imagination, Mother, but it cannot be allowed to run so wild, for you worry about us far too much.' Richard placed her in front of him so that she faced Bethany.

Bethany dipped a curtsey and smiled politely at her. 'I am very pleased to meet you, Ma'am.'

'She's English, definitely! No spies welcome here. Good. What will I do with her, Richard? She will walk far more quickly than I, and I don't know her family. Is she . . . common?' The woman looked her both up and down, but it was with an air of trepidation rather than snobbery.

'I assure you her people are good, pure common folk, with an education and a God-fearing family,' Richard said loudly and laughed. 'I know her father and can vouch for his character.'

'Good! Good! Excellent! I can't abide stuck up servants that are only with you out of circumstance or social gratification. Are you an honest girl? Look me in the eye, mind, as you answer me — I can always tell when one is lying!' The old lady stared at her eyes, so Bethany stared back as she spoke.

'Yes, Ma'am, I am, for James Updale has always told me that nothing catches up with a person as fast as a lie.' Bethany was relieved when the old lady nodded her approval.

Richard turned to speak to Bartholomew. 'You and I must talk, whilst Miss Bethany acquaints herself with Mother.'

'Must we, Dick? I'd far rather acquaint myself, too.' He smirked, but Richard was having none of his nonsense and walked him into the library.

The old lady took Bethany by the elbow and led her towards the staircase. 'Tell me, young Bethany, honestly, do you find my Richard attractive?'

Bethany looked down at this fragile woman with eyes that were both startling and belied a strong spirit still lurking within and answered her surprising question. 'Yes, Ma'am, I do. Is that wrong of me?'

'Absolutely not. He is the most handsome man around. Not pretty like his brother, but handsome, like a man should be. Just as well you didn't lie to me, girl, because I can see it in your eyes. They soften when you look at him. Take care he does not see it. The boy . . . is no fool. Now remember you are here to look after me and I am most demanding, so keep your eyes on your task and we shall be most companionable.'

She started climbing the stairs one at a time leaning on Bethany for support.

'Once we've climbed this mountain you can have them fetch me my hot chocolate.'

'Yes, Ma'am,' Bethany answered, but the lady stopped and looked at her closely.

'Then you can join me. I'll let you have one too, whilst you explain things to me.'

'Explain, ma'am?' Bethany queried.

'That dress suits you, girl.'

'Why thank you, Ma'am.' Bethany blushed.

'Yes, I always liked it when I chose the pattern. Yes, you can explain how you came to be running around the countryside, with my son, in my dress.'

She shook her head. 'Don't worry, girl, I'm not taking the dress from your back, you can keep it. But you will tell Georgina all, for I am not so stupid as some here would think — but I do occasionally lose things, like my sons. That can be most tiresome. Come on now or we shall be having our chocolate on the staircase and that would never do.'

She focussed on climbing to the top landing and Bethany helped her every step of the way, knowing that she was not dealing with a woman who was losing her mind, but one that had sharpened it to perfection.

* * *

Sarah saw Bill Judd before he saw her. He was standing with his group of friends, laughing and bragging as usual, but she couldn't see Kezzie near him. Where was the girl? She'd tan her hide for her when she found her.

Firstly, the little fool had let that Updale strumpet land herself a position with the gentry — what position she could only take a guess at. But, of course that Bethany carried it off with her usual calm decorous manner, 'nought so green as cabbage looking', she told herself.

Meanwhile, the stupid little flirt, her own daughter, was chasing around after farmers! Well, Sarah decided she'd soon put a stop to that. She pushed her way in to the ale hut. Bill saw her wiry figure walking determinedly toward him.

'Hey, lads, look! Me ma-in-law to be has come to wish us luck. Sit yersel' down, Sarah, and we'll celebrate together.' He raised a tankard up to face her, but she brushed it away and looked at him with utter scorn.

'Yer, useless sluggard!' Sarah snapped, which caused a ripple of laughter and gained people's attention.

'Not so useless, I won the competition, woman.' He took a swig of ale.

'The blasted dog won it. You were just stood with the sheep.'

'Language, Sarah, there be gentlemen in here.' His friends laughed, but although Bill's lips formed a smile his eyes looked at hers straight and there was no humour to be had in them.

'What have yer done with me girl?' she asked loudly. Whatever had happened to Kezzie, the blame was going to lay straight at Bill's door, of that Sarah was determined.

'She should be here by now, to celebrate our up and coming wedding and it will be a quick one with no fuss, Sarah, of that I promise yer. So you can forget yer high-faluting ideas. She's marryin' Bill and will come to our farm as soon as we're wed. If yer polite to me ma, she might even let yer visit so long as she's not too busy entertaining.'

He looked around at the crowd smiling, then his expression changed as he looked outside the hut and saw the fair breaking up. 'It's turning dusky outside, where is she?' he asked, but no-one had seen her.

'That's why I'm asking you, you dumb animal. That dog has more sense between its ears than you, Bill Judd!' Sarah shouted at him. He stood up knocking over the table. Sarah stepped back but did not cower from the giant of a man who towered over her.

He raised a fist and a silence fell upon the room.

'Go on hit me, Bill Judd. There are plenty of witnesses to see what a brave man you are when faced with a wisp of a woman. Tell me, is that what you've done to me little Kezzie?' Her eyes watered and Bill looked around him and saw the looks on his drinking companions faces change as he stood there. He let his arm drop down to his side.

'Yer've a mouth on yer like a harlot!' he grumbled.

Sarah gasped and put her gloved hand to her lips. There were murmurings of disapproval in the hut. Sarah looked around at them, pathetically and dewy eyed. She had them in the palm of her hand, and she knew it.

'Won't anyone help to find me girl?' She looked back to Bill. 'Just tell me where she is?'

Bill was visibly shaken. He seemed to be trying to clear his head to lose the blur caused by the ale. 'I don't know what yer talkin' about woman. I told her to make herself presentable and meet me here . . . I don't know why she didn't come . . . '

People were staring at him, he didn't understand why, and Sarah enjoyed his confusion. If her girl had done something stupid with him, he'd pay now and Kezzie would when she got her back home, but this was her chance to strike back at the Judds.

She'd been one once, but they slighted her when she married a man for love. How was she to know he'd go and get himself killed in the war? No, she'd see old Ma Judd suffer like she had.

'Where did yer leave her, Bill and why did she have to make herself presentable? She was pressed all pretty when last I saw her.' Her voice had softened with honey sweetness, in stark contrast to the previous insults.

He swayed slightly.

'She was in the alley, Sarah . . . we'd been celebratin',' he turned to the crowd that had gathered, 'yer know.' He winked at them, boasting, 'Well we're to wed! She has me child already!'

Sarah let out a scream and fell into a

faint. She was caught by strong arms. 'Find my poor baby! Please, bring her back to me and restrain that beast! He's violated my girl!'

She pointed at him accusingly. 'No wonder he separated her from her friend on the moor road, leaving poor Bethany Updale to wander on alone.'

She knew the Updale boys were in the hut and saw them stand as they slammed their tankards down on the table.

'Don't twist things, you old witch,' Bill stuttered as some of the men stood up and faced him. 'The girl's boot had ripped, I fixed it so as she could make her way back. She knew the way and Kez was keen for us to be alone, like. They can vouch for that.' He pointed to his friends.

'Aye, that's true. She weren't best pleased when you dropped her like, in the fairground, and got on with the competition.'

Sarah muttered to herself, then forced out the words, 'What man worth his salt leaves young maids on their own in these parts. The man's an animal!' Sarah led her lids flutter closed, falling into the arms of one of the older men. She could just see Bill being manhandled by a group of men and being taken outside.

The Updales followed on behind. A group of farmers organised themselves into a search party outside. Bill'll get a good kicking for sure, but where was her Kezzie? Underneath Sarah's satisfaction, a genuine concern was rising within her.

Why hadn't she come to her ma when they'd raised their voices? Suddenly, she was filled with a sense of foreboding, bordering on blind panic. What if they can't find her? Where was her baby? She let out a cry, shouting her daughter's name and ran from the hut, calling her, but her Kezzie didn't reply.

8

'Adam, they're calling for more, they love me!' Kezzie swung around, throwing her arms around his neck and kissed him passionately on his lips.

Pulling away, reluctantly, he whispered to her, 'You'd better go on once more, my little flower. Never disappoint your audience!'

She did not hesitate, but ran back to where she truly belonged on centre stage, even if it was a makeshift one in a market town.

Kezzie waved at him as she climbed back up the stairs to the wooden flooring. A ripple of applause greeted her as she skipped on. She was like a child, having fun, being adored. Her curls, like her, had a natural spring to them whenever she performed. Even though she was heavy with child, the ruffled flounces of her colourful costume hid her firm bump.

Sometimes, when she was hot, and sweating in the sun's heat, the fabric clung to her body, but unaware she continued singing or acting absorbing the attention of the crowd. Adam was never jealous. She was a thing of beauty in its prime and like all things beautiful should be enjoyed. It was only when beauty faded, and had had its day did it belong in the shade.

In his opinion, anyway, he knew he would never lose his beauty because he felt that his was an internal youth, of attitude and thought that would never fade. Kezzie's was an outer beauty and therefore she needed to enjoy it to the full whilst she could. Then, when she faded her memories would keep her warm.

Her energy seemed to defy nature and grow with the child rather than wane. Adam knew he had set a wild flower free.

'She's the best thing this ram-shackle group has picked up along the way,' said Jake as he leaned against a large drum, used by the jester.

'Why do you think I took her on?' Adam answered, with a big smile on his face.

'Because Adam needed a willing and grateful Eve to keep him warm through the long and lonely winter nights.' Jake watched him. Adam sensed the man's desire for her, but she was a natural tease. There would never be a cold night for Kezzie so long as her looks held up. She was a survivor, who had never once mentioned her poor mama, or the father of her child.

'That as well, I suppose if I'm honest, which I am always. She'll pass us all up somewhere along the line, Jake, but for now she attracts people and their hard earned money. We all gain from our union.' Adam slapped his friend on the back. 'Go juggle, man, and keep your eyes off my woman!'

'Can't control my eyes, Adam, but I shall everything else.'

Kezzie returned smiling at Jake as he passed by her, her bounce not quite as keen as it had been, but she had just finished her fourth show of the day.

'You were . . . ' Adam offered her a hand, but she knocked it to the side, made a bolt for behind the stage and doubled up. 'Adam . . . I feel sick . . . I have pains . . . I . . . '

Adam was there in a second. He gave orders for someone to cover his act whilst he lifted Kezzie away from the crowd to the tent they had shared for three nights. 'You are going to have a child, little one. Don't worry, Adam will help, Adam knows how it's done!' he said and tried to comfort her.

'But he ain't done it for himself, has he? I want Ma! Where's my mama? I want Mama! I . . . I . . . ' Kezzie doubled over.

Adam supported her, he knew her time had come and the girl was about to be a mother herself. It was time for her to grow up and be responsible for another life. Now, slowly she would start to fade as nature determined she would, but not straight away, slowly.

He wondered how this would change her character, only time would tell, and Adam had plenty of that, for each day was a new adventure. Tomorrow another life would share it with him, and that, he thought, would be special enough.

* * *

Bethany washed Georgina and dressed her ready for her morning walk. It was not very far before she would take to her basket chair and then she would be wheeled to the newly-built conservatory with its myriad of green plants and ornate statues. Then she would read to her and chat aimlessly before once more returning for a nap.

It was then and only then she could share a few special hours with Richard planning the progress of the work on the east wing. That alone was a full-time occupation for as soon as one job was finished another one had to begin.

Richard entered the conservatory and looked at his mother. 'Mama, I need

Bethany for a few hours. Father has agreed to sit with you awhile until she returns.'

'Well, what am I to say, Richard? Won't Bartholomew do? I haven't seen him today.' Her vacant look as she glanced from one to another hurt Richard deeply, Bethany could tell.

'Bartholomew returned to London four months ago, Mama. He is expected back by Christmas.' Richard stroked his mother's arm gently.

'Richard would you like a hound? Or do you think I look like one!' His mother was flustered. Her moods could swing at the drop of a pin; it was confusing at times as she would forget things so easily and quickly, then she'd reminisce at length about her childhood.

The lady was clearly ailing and failing, but it came and it went. Bethany stayed calm and tried to soothe her when she became aware of it herself and cried. There was nothing to be done, just be kind and watchful, but

Richard felt sad when it happened. He loved his mother.

Richard stopped instantly. 'Neither, Mama.'

'I forgot for a moment, that is all. Is it odd I should wish to have my son by my side? No, not at all! So don't look at me that way. I'll see him at dinner, then.' She looked from one to the other as they stood silent for a moment.

'At Christmas dinner, ma'am,' Bethany corrected her gently.

'Yes, yes, that's what I said. Oh, go and play, children, your pranks are tiring. Send me my husband. I hope he has not gone off somewhere, too.'

They looked at each other and left in silence. Once on their own she slipped her hand in his and squeezed it gently; he held it firmly and looked at her, 'Whatever would we do without you?' he asked.

'You don't have to,' she answered and smiled at him.

'No, you're right, I don't,' he said, and kissed her hand.

Bethany had become accustomed to these small affectionate gestures, they never failed to brighten her spirits and warm her heart. 'Come, you are going to learn to ride with me.'

'Me?' she queried.

'Yes, you, ride!' He laughed at her surprised expression and presented her with a riding outfit. 'Go and change, I'll fetch the horse . . . and when you join me, smile.'

She watched him run off to the stable and wondered whatever would happen next. She would not have long to find out.

* * *

Kezzie screamed loudly and tore at Adam's clothes with her hands; she was sweating profusely and bellowing. Things, Adam knew, were not going well. He worked away silently despite the woman's attacks and tried to turn the baby around; he sensed it was not as it should be.

Against her protestations and with an onlooking worried group of friends, he decided to act according to his instincts. Adam had always trusted them before, so why not now. He had nothing to lose because if he let things carry on the way they were she and the baby could be dead.

He waited for her next push and she screamed like a banshee as he helped the baby to come, freeing the cord around its neck. It was born thus, in a moment of excruciating pain. The child, a baby boy was dragged into the world. He had saved the child and the likelihood was that Kezzie would recover.

The women took over and the baby was cleaned and returned to its mama, who lay sobbing on the soiled blankets, hardly wanting to touch the new life lying next to her at all. She cried for her own mama, repeatedly. The child, a boy, cried also by its mama's side, but the mama was too lost in her own distress to care.

Adam left the smell and heat of the tent and found the fresh cold air outside. He breathed deeply and washed himself in the cold stream, holding his head in his hand. It throbbed like a hammer was pounding at his brains from inside his skull. He had nearly lost both their lives.

Exhausted, he fell to the floor. What had he done? What had he been thinking of to take on a pregnant girl? His freedom, the one thing he valued before all else ever since he had escaped the cells, even now he shuddered at the thought. He could still feel the cold dank floor, the kickings he had received from the guards and the pungent sickening smell.

The birth smell had brought it all back to him, that and his head pounding. It was a place he never would return to. He would rather die on the open road, loving life and breathing fresh air, not owing a soul anything — money, time or love. His future, it all seemed to have been swallowed up in the girl's wails, her curses and cries.

He dragged himself up to his feet and took himself off to his wagon and slept peacefully. Tomorrow he would face the day anew.

An onlooker had heard the noises and screams that emanated from the tent, Kezzie's desperate cries. Whoever the child was, the woman realised that she was crying out for her mama, and the cries had touched the older woman's heart.

She had waited for the girl to be left in the tent alone with her babe. Blankets were removed by the players' women, it was then that she poked her head inside the canvas flap.

'Well, well, what have we here?' she asked aloud, but did not step inside; she listening in case someone should return. She did not know these people and her concern may not be welcomed.

'Tell me dear, who is your mama? Does she still live? Can I fetch her for you?'

Kezzie tried to lift her head to see who it was that spoke. Everything ached and they had left her, vulnerable. Her body felt as though it did not belong to her anymore. Here, a stranger was staring at her prone body; it felt broken. She glanced at the bundle which lay alongside her. What had it done to her? She wondered.

'Can you hear me, lovely?' the voice asked her.

'Yes, she does still live, I hope, but she lives in Beckmere. Her name is Sarah Wright, and I miss her. I wish she were here,' Kezzie sobbed uncontrollably.

'You'll be stayin' here a few days; perhaps I could get a message to her. Would that make you happy?' She could hear voices approaching and was eager to be gone.

'Yes . . . ' Kezzie blubbed, and paused while she tried to think straight through her misery and pain.

The woman heard, yes, the word was enough and ran off.

Kezzie fought to regain her composure, then added, ' . . . but she must never know where I am, or what I've done with myself, or I shall be shamed for life!' Kezzie answered, but when she looked up it was Jake's face whom she saw.

'Now, who would that be you're talking to? Oh, look, lass, he's beautiful. What are yer goin' to call him?'

She let her head flop back, convinced she had been dreaming. Call him? Her head ached so much. What did she care what he was called! She sighed. 'Ask Adam, he is full of ideas, he'll know,' then she thought for a moment, 'Cain, he shall be called Cain.'

She chuckled then slept, unaware that Jake had picked the boy up, wrapped in the shawl, and was hugging him to his body, keeping the baby warm and humming until the fractious child settled to sleep.

'Don't worry, little one, you shall be called Abel, yes, you're an Abel, not a Cain.'

* * *

Sarah walked the mile to the village. She did it almost in a trance. She'd thought about moving, but where would her baby come to find her should she return? No she had to stay in Beckmere, but the looks of pity of hatred she received made her flesh crawl.

She had once walked proudly along this road, her beautiful daughter by her side. The prettiest of girls in the neighbourhood, but she had gone to the fair on that fateful day and had never been seen again, shamed by the brute of a man, Judd. His family hated her, for their finest son had now gone also.

At least they knew where he was. He'd taken the King's shilling to avoid being arrested, or beaten up again by the Updale boys for leaving their Bethany alone on the moor road. Mind, the girl had done well from it.

At least Bill Judd stood a fighting chance in the army, but he'd never said what had become of her lovely Kezzie. She'd vanished like the wind. Even now, her mama did not know when the tears would come upon her or where.

People might say she was going mad, but grief affects folk differently, and she grieved for the void that Kezzie's absence had left and the uncertainty, was she alive or dead? Sarah sniffed as she approached the main street.

A small group of people had gathered by a cart in front of the village shop. As she approached, Isadora Updale ran to greet her. Funny, Sarah had often thought, of all the people in the village that she had given reason to have been happy at Sarah's miserable state of affairs she thought old Isadora would be head of the list, but she wasn't. The woman had soothed her, fed her when she was in a state of shock and had her sons on constant vigil for any news of the girl.

'Sarah, Sarah we have news for you. Dry your tears, love, for Kezzie lives!'

Instantly, Sarah's head shot up high.

'Where? Tell me where my baby is?'

Isadora told her what the woman, who had come to the poorhouse in search of news of a Sarah Wright, had told her.

'I must go to her straight away!' Sarah said urgently, her thin body trembling with anticipation.

'You wait here, Sarah, I'll fetch James and the cart. We can't have you running around the countryside on your own.' She hugged Sarah to her. 'Don't worry, lass. Whatever the outcome, we'll fetch her back for you. You'll be a family again.'

Sarah's eyes glistened. 'Oh, I'll have the little scrap of hers, no matter what the father was. I just want me baby back.'

Isadora hugged her and saw the look on a few faces of the village women who had overheard their conversation as they had slowly passed by.

'Aye, we'll look after them both, like good Christian folk!' Isadora said the words firmly and the other two women raised an eyebrow or two as they walked briskly off to spread the good news.

Kezzie had a child out of wedlock, and was coming back to her distraught mother. Isadora wondered how long it would take word to get back to Bill's ma. Not long, she guessed, which was how long they had to be on their way and away before trouble started all over again.

* * *

'Richard, it's so much fun. You are so lucky to have done this for so many years.' Bethany shouted over to him as they almost cantered across the open moor road. He pulled her reins and slowed the horses to a steady walk.

'Is there nothing you are not naturally gifted at?' he said to her and grinned warmly.

'Many things, but I shall not tell you what they are for it is up to you to find them out,' she teased him.

'Bethany, Mama is not well.' His demeanour changed instantly. 'I feel we will lose her soon enough, but I want you to stay here. Tell me that you enjoy my company and will gladly stay.' He looked at her.

'I am not sure that I should . . . ' She averted her eyes from his.

'There! I have found out already!' he said and laughed. 'You lie! You are terrible at it. You know perfectly well that it is your greatest desire to stay here . . . with me.'

'You presume too much, sir,' she answered him, trying to keep the smile from her face.

'Then let me presume that if I ask you to marry me, you would answer in the affirmative?' He leaned close to her.

'Then I suggest, sir, you ask me outright and then you would not have to presume at all, you would know for sure!' she replied quickly and dared herself to kick the horse on slightly so that it went into a rising trot.

She heard him laugh and his horse

approaching, but in the distance she saw a familiar figure sitting upon the cart.

'James!' she shouted, and rode to greet him, realising he was not alone.

9

Bethany did not know if Richard was teasing her, or if he was seriously considering proposing to her. She dared herself to imagine him actually asking her to marry him. She laughed at the thought. They had become good friends and as they discussed the building and its needs, he talked openly with her about many things — his mother and father and the merchant shop his father had owned for years.

It was Richard, though, who had served in France and, although being sent home injured, had secured the family's wealth. He had put it down to being in the right place at the right time. Then his aunt had left the old house to her favourite nephew. Their future was then properly secured.

Richard had even briefly discussed his injury that had left him with a scar upon his chest where a bullet nearly took his life away, but marriage — that was something she had not thought possible. However, seeing James with two familiar faces looking at her from the back of the cart, who she now realised were Isadora and Sarah, she pushed her thoughts to the back of her mind and rode straight over toward them.

'Well, look at you, girl! You're a pretty sight for sore eyes if ever I've seen one!' James said out loud, but received a sharp dig in the ribs from Isadora, for being less than tactful, as Sarah was obviously in an emotional state.

'Sarah, whatever is the matter?' Bethany asked as she saw the concern on Isadora's face and Sarah's agitated manner. 'Has something else happened?'

Sarah answered eagerly, with moist eyes and a trembling lip. 'They've found my Kezzie. She's been kidnapped by those touring players!' Sarah said angrily, her fists clenched in rage.

Richard rode alongside of the cart. Bethany could tell by his expression that he had heard what she had said.

'Are you sure of your facts, ma'am?' he asked, and looked at James for confirmation of it.

'We know she has been seen with them, and within the last few days she has had a child, but we don't know if her presence there was willing, or not. We are going to find out now. Would you care to join us, sir, for I fear things could get out of hand if she does not welcome our arrival?' James looked at him earnestly and winked at Bethany.

'Or if Sarah's fears are founded, but I doubt this,' he glanced back at the women, 'for Kezzie is a resourceful girl and I'm sure she would have found some way of alerting people to her plight, as they cannot have left the country all this time.' James looked sternly at Sarah.

'Then why would she not send word to her mamma?' Sarah asked, her manner bemused.

‘For fear of retribution I would suggest. The girl was pregnant!’ James’ voice was not unkind, but he obviously did not want wild accusations being made, unfounded.

‘Of course we will, James. You carry on and we’ll ride ahead and see what is occurring there. If she is being held against her will, Mrs Wright, I will deal with it. If not,’ he glanced at James, ‘then you will have to accept that, but at least you will know at last where she is . . . and why.’

Sarah nodded. ‘I want my baby back, even if she has one of her own.’

‘If that is your wish, then we will tell her of it, if we find her there still. Players do move on,’ Richard said, trying to make the truth sound softer than the reality that she may not be where she was last seen.

‘Please, find her!’ Sarah pleaded. ‘Don’t go scaring her off. I want my daughter back; even if she’s not been treated as a lady should. Bethany, you know her, she’ll not run from you. Tell her I'll be right with her. No matter what has been going on.'

Sarah looked pale and desperate and Bethany could not have imagined such a once overly proud woman so humbled by events. She had always been quite strict with Kezzie, expecting her to rise above her station in life, not sink away below it.

'I will, Sarah,' she answered, and looked to Richard. They rode off together.

Bethany was a little unsteady on the horse and gasped as they made the steep descent into the neighbouring vale. It felt to her as if she would slip down the animal's neck and arrive in an unruly heap at the bottom of the bank.

'Lean backwards, Bethany, not forwards, or you'll come off!' Richard shouted to her, but she found she had instinctively done it. The horse seemed to know where it was going, so she kept a firm hold on the reins and breathed deeply.

If she didn't panic then the horse

would sense her calm.

It was what she hoped would happen anyway.

Her excitement grew as she saw the covered wagons still in the village. Bethany remembered the same vehicles passing her by the night Kezzie mysteriously disappeared.

She had been riddled with guilt afterwards for she knew Kez had been having *relations* with someone other than Bill. Both she and Richard saw them. But what good would it have done to say so.

Her name had been dragged through the dirt over her behaviour with Bill, and the unborn child she had already carried. Bethany did not know if she had thrown herself at the first line of escape — the players, or if she had run away by herself, but whatever her fate had been, Kezzie had taken it in her own hands, and she was a survivor.

She had left Bethany to her own devices, not knowing how near death she had come in the woods. Bill Judd had paid for his ill treatment of them both. Justice on that score had been most severe. Bethany would have settled for an apology at his callous desertion of her on the moor, but her adoptive brothers had always said she was too soft.

They were outraged, and she had even heard a rumour that they put the King's Shilling in Bill's tankard so he had accepted it without knowing.

She hoped they had not been so devious, but none would tell her the truth of it. Isadora had told her to stay at the dowager's house; it still carried the name locally, and not to venture near the Judd farm on her own. Times were not easy with two grieving women at war with each other in such a small community, but Isadora said peace would return, one day.

Richard came alongside her as they entered the village. He left the horses tethered and grazing on the common land and walked with Bethany to one of the covered wagons.

Bethany saw an actor, one of the players, seemingly packing up his wagon. Richard approached him, but Bethany cupped his elbow with her gloved hand before he neared.

'What is it? Don't be afraid, you are with me.' Richard put a protective hand on hers.

She looked at him touched by his comment as he was always there to reassure her. 'His boots, they're the same as the ones we saw . . . you know, with Kezzie's. The buckles shine so!'

He nodded, knowing that she was right. This handsome young man was the one who had been with Kezzie in the workshop.

'Excuse me, but I wonder if you could help us?' Richard said to the man, who looked at them quickly, then raised an eyebrow.

'That would depend on what it is that you want, sir . . . ma'am.' He bowed in a theatrical manner and Bethany could see how easy it would be for him to charm a young girl with his fancy ways. So different to Bill Judd, that was for sure.

'We're looking for a friend of ours who appears to have lost her way. Her name is Kezzie and she has been seen in this village.' Richard's voice had changed, although polite it was firm. He spoke as if he knew fine well that she had been with him, or at least seen with him.

'Why would you be wanting to meet up again with this 'friend', sir, if she has lost her way?' He faced Richard squarely; he was holding the horse's bridle in his hand and Bethany was worried that the man may become violent.

'She is my friend and we fear she left home because she had found herself in a frightening situation. We want to take her back home to be with her mother, who has missed her sorely. It is where she belongs, sir.' Bethany was almost inching between the two of them.

The man smiled broadly, 'It's all right, miss! I'll take you to her, but I must warn you, 'young and innocent' isn't quite the way she has been behaving these last few days. Since becoming a mother herself, her more forthright nature has been unleashed.'

Richard grabbed the man's arm. 'Answer me this, man. Did you take the girl against her will? In any way?'

He glared at Richard. 'Listen to me, sir. The girl came to me willingly. I looked after her when the lout who had made her pregnant drank ale and bragged with his friend.' The man looked down at Richard's hand. 'Please remove that. I am in no way provoking you, neither do I intend to. I have done nothing that is wrong. I merely assisted a maiden in distress.'

'Blast you! Have you no respect or are you no more than a mere animal. Most would argue that that was immoral, sir!' Richard said quietly to him. Bethany looked away.

'My name is Adam. What I do is of no concern to you if it does not hurt or damage anything that is yours. We are all kinds of animals, sir. Now, I think, it is you who embarrasses the lady. Now, do you wish to see Kezzie or not?'

He calmly looked from her to Richard. His manner was so confident and smooth that Bethany could see Richard was controlling his temper as he had so often with Bartholomew.

His brother also had the gift of the tongue, but Bethany had suspected was not hero material, unless he talked the enemy into submission.

'If it is against the law, then you are wrong, sir, it indeed would be my concern!' Richard was standing his ground.

'Yes, on that I concede, but I have helped your 'willing' friend through a very difficult time. Please come this way.'

He led them behind the wagon to another one that had solid sides and an arched roof. It looked to Bethany like a little narrow cottage on wheels. As they approached Bethany heard Kezzie's irate voice clearly.

'The swine wants to leave me here! That's what it is. I have a child and now I'm not good enough for him. He knows too well I'm a better actor than he any day of the week!' Her voice was almost at screaming pitch.

'You have a child now! He needs you. You can't face another long journey so soon. Listen to sense, lass. You're not strong enough. You lost a lot of blood, Kez. Listen, I'll stay behind with you. You don't need Adam. He's a great man, but you can't keep a spirit like him tied down, he needs to be free or he'll perish. Let him be free. He loves you, Kezzie, but not just you, Adam loves life and everyone. He's incapable of loving just one woman . . . unlike me. I want to settle down. I'd love a family and . . . I love you . . . ' The man's voice was softly spoken, humble even as it trailed off.

There was a pause, 'You?' Kezzie's voice asked gently as if the bitterness had been knocked out of it.

Adam stepped back. 'Excuse me, if I

don't introduce you myself, but her aim is improving each time my head appears.' He bowed low and returned to his horse and wagon.

Bethany peeped inside the wagon. She saw a pale looking Kez staring at a large built man who was hugging a tiny bundle in his arms lovingly. Kezzie flung her arms around his neck and he hugged her with is free one. Bethany looked on in awe. This girl — woman, seemed to have men falling for her every time she turned from one, there was another there.

'Can I help you?' the man said gruffly, and Kezzie looked around to see who he was speaking to.

'Bethany! Bethany!' she cried out and ran to her. 'However did you find me?'

'A woman took word to your mother.' Bethany watched her friend's face freeze somewhere between laughter and tears.

'Is she here?' the girl asked nervously.

'She will be soon, Kez. She wants you back, babe and all.'

Kezzie put her hand to her mouth. 'She knows? What about Bill, he'll be out for my blood.' Kezzie looked at Jake and the baby.

'No, he won't because he's joined the army. But you'll have to stay clear of his ma.' Bethany stepped back as Kezzie wrapped herself in her shawl and stepped down from the wagon. She flung her arms around Bethany.

'Forgive me, Beth. I've been a fool.'

Bethany looked at Richard over her friend's shoulder. She felt strangely detached from the girl's display of affection. She just did not know if it was genuine. Richard shrugged his shoulders as if he understood her thoughts.

Bethany patted her back, which Kezzie seemed to take as a sign that all was well between them.

'Kezzie!' the shout from the approaching wagon startled the girl. Mother and daughter ran to each other and were at once wrapped in each other's embrace.

Bethany smiled at Jake and looked at

the baby's peaceful face, as it lay safe in his strong arms, 'I'll see he's kept well. My own wife died in childbirth. I'll see this little might has a life.' He winked at Bethany, and she realised he understood what Kezzie was, but his heart was in love with the babe.

10

Richard and Bethany walked to the inn with James and Isadora. Bethany linked arms with Isadora who looked really happy to have them all with her.

'You look like a real lady, lass,' Isadora whispered to her.

'Well, they seem to have reconciled themselves,' Richard commented as he saw mother and daughter in a tight embrace. His expression changed when he saw Adam wave to them as he boldly took his wagon out of the village.

'He has no responsibilities in life, a wastrel.' Richard shook his head.

'Each to his own, Dick,' James said. 'Some choose to live and die alone.'

'So long as they take what they want along the way,' Isadora added.

'Oh, I think whatever he has had, has been freely given,' James added as they all sat down at a table in the bay of the window. Richard ordered some food to eat and drinks.

'So how are things going up at the old house?' Isadora said. 'We haven't seen your ma at the poor-house for a few weeks. Mind you, she's been very generous. They've never had it so good. It's a lot warmer and cleaner in there since her rules were introduced. Not so many going down with the sniffles and agues.' Isadora winked at Bethany, who was pleased to see her look so well and happy. 'You're lookin' grand, lass. The air up there must suit you.'

'Aye, somethin' does!' James said and chuckled. He took a welcome drink of ale, but looked at Richard, winking cheekily at him.

'Pa, behave yourself, man. You'll embarrass Bethany,' Isadora rebuked him.

'On the contrary; I was trying to convince Bethany of the same thing as we rode over here, but alas, she does not take me seriously.' Richard shrugged his shoulders.

Bethany was about to sip her drink when he spoke. She stopped and looked at him. All eyes were watching her. 'I love the house and the air there. They work wonders for one's complexion.' She watched their surprised faces.

Richard glanced out of the window; his smile vanished in a trice. He ran out of the inn, closely followed by James who had instinctively followed Richard's swift reaction.

'Stay in here, stay safe, woman,' he shouted the orders to Isadora.

'Whatever has happened?' Bethany stood up looking out of the window. 'Oh, no! Will this business never be settled?' She made her way to the back of the inn, leaving Isadora staring in disbelief at the scene outside.

'So yer thought that yer could take me grandson away as well as me Bill, did yer? Well, woman, yer mistaken, because that there's Bill's child and we'll bring him up, not that harlot! Give him over, to us now!' The pistols wavered in her hands.

Ma Judd was sat atop an old baker's cart. Her other son held it steady, but she had a pistol in each hand. One was pointed at Kezzie the other at Richard and James as they ran out into the street. Bethany ran out, of the back of the inn, unseen.

'Take care, woman. What good would you be to any babe if you're arrested for injuring folks,' James' voice was loud and clear.

'Stay out of this, Updale. Your boys did enough when they tricked my Bill into the army. Just go and get the babe and bring it here to me and no more will be said nor done. She don't want a child hanging around her heels, she can't take it on stage with her, can she?' Her words were slurred and it was obvious that she'd been drinking.

Bethany ran around the side of the inn and skirted the shadows of the buildings until she was level with Ma Judd's cart. 'You're right there, Mrs Judd. She has acted like a harlot.'

One of the pistols was sighted at her.

'What you doin' here you live in the dowager's ruin, don't yer? You've no business with the common folk anymore.'

Bethany ignored her comments and calmly continued. 'She's not only been with Bill, Mrs Judd. She'd been with the actor too. How do you know that baby is Bill's? You Judds have fair or ginger hair, the baby has black hair. I doubt he's Bill's!' Bethany spoke loud and clearly.

'How dare you!' Kezzie shouted, but she was silenced as Bethany pulled a piece of ribbon from her pocket and held it high in the air.

'Remember this, Kez? Can you also remember where you lost it?' She held up the pale blue ribbon that matched Kezzie's eyes. Bethany had carried it with her ever since her friend disappeared as a reminder of what can happen when a girl loses everything dear to her, her mother, her home and her self respect.

In her own way she had grieved for

the loss of a friend, but over time had come to accept that the friend had never been a true one, not even letting her own mother know that she was safe.

'You trollop!' Ma Judd lowered the pistols, her arms hanging by her sides, 'And my boy was going to marry you — for that!' she pointed to the bundle still held protectively in Jake's arms.

'Come on, Ma, she ain't worth it,' her son said and, as the woman sank back on to the seat, he turned the cart around and took her away.

Bethany walked boldly forward. The villagers had heard her words. Kezzie looked around her, shame-faced.

'Did you have to do that to me?' Kezzie asked under her breath. Her mother still stood by her side although she was more aware of the disapproving looks people were giving them.

'Yes!' she said bluntly. 'For how else were you going to remove her desire to have your child?' Bethany placed the ribbon in Kezzie's hand. 'Whoever else's he is, he is your child for sure.'

'Bethany!' Kezzie gasped.

'You've found another good man, Kez,' Bethany looked at Jake, 'Try and hang on to this one.' She left her, staring at the ribbon, and returned to Richard.

'That was both brave and downright stupid, woman!' He wrapped his arms around her. 'Don't ever do anything like that again.' Without caring who saw them he kissed her full on the mouth.

James and Isadora stood and watched them for a few moments until they separated.

'James, I wish to marry your daughter,' Richard said. 'But first, before I make it official, I must return to my parents who will be thinking we have eloped already, as this tide has been overly long. If you'll excuse me . . . '

James caught hold of his sleeve. 'Just a minute, lad.' He looked at Bethany, 'Are you willing for this match to go ahead, lass?'

She looked at him and smiled. 'I'll let

you know when he asks 'me'.' She turned away boldly, but not before winking discreetly at Isadora, who already knew the answer.

'Leave them be, James,' she told her husband. 'They'll sort it out soon enough.'

They rode back up the steep bank together and across the flat moor road before he turned off and took them back down the trail that led into the forest on the edge of the estate.

As they approached the buildings the path widened and they could ride side by side. He took her horse's reins in his hand and dismounted. He tethered both animals to a tree and helped Bethany down.

'I thought we had to get back in a hurry,' Bethany said, when he made no attempt to release his hold on her sides as her feet firmly met solid ground.

'Bethany, I am asking 'you' not your father. Will you marry me?' he kissed her lips tenderly.

'Richard, tell me something first before I answer.'

He sighed and looked into her eyes. 'What is that, Miss Bethany?'

'What happens when your home is finished and there is no more to be done with it? Won't you be bored with it, and with me? Have you really thought this through, looked at the future and not just the present?' Bethany held his arms in hers.

'Woman, do you know how to say, yes, or not?' Richard looked at her with what she hoped was only mock despair.

'Yes!' she said, and smiled.

'You think too much, woman. Live for the day for tomorrow is in God's hands not ours!'

'You preach, sir.'

'When the house is done, I'll start improving the workings of the farm. Once that is finished then I'll rebuild the workers' quarters and so on . . . ' He kissed her again, this time with more urgency. 'I promise I shall never tire of you unless you keep asking annoying questions. Answer me, Bethany, do you love me?'

She stroked his hair. 'Yes,' was her answer, 'to both questions.'

He swung her in his arms and kissed her repeatedly. Her bonnet came loose and fell to the floor. Their laughter grew.

'Well, isn't this an unusual sight!' Bartholomew's voice stopped them mid-swing. The moment of magic was shattered.

'So, you two have been behaving like rabbits in the wild. I suspected it, but did not think my little brother had it in him. Too boring, but not too predictable it would seem.'

'I'm used to your insults, Bartholomew, but you do not insult Bethany. She is to be my wife and not spoken of in such a way.' Richard said as he picked up Bethany's bonnet and handed it to her.

Richard was rising to his bait. He rarely did, but Bethany knew he would not have him throw such insults at her.

'Just as well then that I didn't blow your brains out on that fateful day when you both met,' he smiled, as both of them were taken aback that he had known what he had hit with his wild shot. 'It took a while to figure it all out, but when Mama told me she'd always loved that dress, and you came with meagre possessions, ill befitting a lady's companion, I realised I had bagged a bird.

'So what have you been doing to him young Beth? Bribery, blackmail or charming him! He's gullible and honourable — I'm neither.' Bartholomew looked down at them from his superior mount.

'You take me for a fool, Bart. I would not fall for such a wench as that. Bethany has done nothing other than fulfil her role here perfectly, with Mama.' Richard held Bethany's hand.

'How can you be a hero, without honour?' Bethany asked.

'Dear child, heroes with honour are the dead ones, I still live. You figure out the detail however you wish to interpret it.' He turned to Richard and swayed slightly. 'Little brother, it appears I need your help sooner than I thought I would.'

'Your funds were supposed to last until Christmas, Bartholomew. Even you can't have gone through them so soon!' Richard sounded angry, but as he approached Bartholomew he realised something was wrong with him, other than his need to tease and toy with people. He was holding his side in a firm grip.

'I met up with some old friends, Richard. They remembered an equally old debt, and were quite insistent that I pay them. Apparently, the tales of my heroism had spread further afield and, once they heard the good news, they sought to renew our acquaintance.'

'Good God, man, you're injured.' Richard mounted his horse. 'Bethany, ride the other side of him. Together we shall help him to return home.' They moved on and it soon became apparent that Bartholomew was in a great deal of pain.

'This really is good of you, Richard. I came the back way. If anyone insists upon my returning with them to the debtors' gaol in York, I would be obliged it you would decline their offer. I swear, I'll amend my ways, honestly!'

Richard and Bethany looked at each other, neither said a word.

Once inside the courtyard, they were helped by the blacksmith, who eased Bartholomew out of his saddle, supporting the man's weight.

'There you are! You children play far too long!'

'Mama, what are you doing out here?' Bethany could hear the note of alarm in Richard's voice; she went straight to the old lady, who was huddled in her shawl.

'There now, I told you Bartholomew was coming home to me. You didn't believe me, did you? Look, he's so tired after his journey. Richard see to your brother, he must rest, fighting all those nasty people.'

She shook her head, but Bethany carefully steered her back into the house whilst Richard saw to Bartholomew. What had been the happiest moment of her life had been turned upside down, but she knew in time it would return to her once more.

The blacksmith carried Bartholomew bodily up to his bedchamber and helped Richard to remove his coat.

'Thank you, Henry. I'll manage now.' Richard said as he stared at the prone figure lying on the bed, groaning as he shifted his weight.

'Sir, a man, one of those fair types, asked if I could give him a hand with his wagon down the moor road. The wheel hit something and needs fixing. Do you mind if I go?' Henry asked.

'No.' Richard wasn't really paying much attention to him; his focus was fixed on Bartholomew. 'Make sure that Mister Bartholomew's horse is stabled and store his tack in the back of the stall. And Henry, if anyone asks, you've been working, no time to see neither anything nor anyone.'

'Aye, sir.' Henry nodded and left.

Richard pulled his brother's shirt up over his chest and saw his bruised torso.

'You took a kicking, for sure.' For once there was no witty reply.

'I've made a real mess of things, Richard. You can mock me if you like, I know more than you how much I deserve it. I've always envied that boring practicality you have. You stick doggedly to whatever it is you're doing and somehow it works. You even caught the pretty lady this time.' He sighed deeply, as Richard felt his ribs. 'Is nothing sacred?' he asked.

'She is a lady, remember that. Born to commoners or not, but she is still a lady and should be treated with respect by you, Bartholomew. No soldiers' course jokes around her.' Richard decided that his ribs were fine, but he was bruised and sore and, as always, he did not cope with pain well. He looked at his crestfallen brother. 'How much do you owe this time?'

'It is not a matter of money, Richard. I made that up for the benefit of your fiancée. Congratulations. It's a firing squad that I'm trying to keep one step ahead of. I . . . I . . . really have made a bad judgement this time. You see, when I came back I didn't exactly tell you all the truth. The battle that was supposed to have been my finest hour didn't happen quite as I related the story to Mother and Father. You see, I charged when they came at us, but unfortunately, in the wrong direction.' He looked at Richard who was struggling to come to terms with the gravity of his words.

'You mean you . . . ran!' Richard could hardly bring himself to say the words.

'Yes, Richard, I do. I'm a coward . . . not a hero. I leave that sort of thing to those who can do it — like you.' He looked directly at him. 'Richard, I was panic stricken. The whole of Napoleon's army seemed to be marching straight at me, shouting and drumming. Oh God, Richard, help me get away, or I'll be shot! Ask yourself, could you live with that thought?'

Richard spun around running a hand

through his hair. 'Where can you run, man?'

'Anywhere, I just need a disguise, some cash and anonymity. I need to blend with the crowd, lose myself — be looked upon, but not seen . . . as me, a gentleman, a solider.'

'A coward. How many men did you leave with no direction to be hacked to pieces by the enemy, whilst you turned tail, man?'

'Hate me if you must. Richard, I didn't intend to run away, but the noise, the smell, the blood and gore — man, I was scared rigid. I'm just not a soldier. I didn't know what to do and everyone was shouting at me, asking me. What could I do? I've not been trained for that sort of thing!' Bartholomew looked at him, obviously more distraught about his own position than anyone else's.

'You could have tried, Bartholomew, and fought like every other man and boy on the field. Do you not think they were scared too? What makes you so special and precious?' He shook his head. 'They'll be here in no time. I'll send some food up. Rest, whilst I think this through. Bart, for once I cannot begin to know what to think about you. You're a fool!' Richard stepped towards the door. 'Don't try taking the honourable way out, for you'd kill your parents also.'

'As if I would,' Bartholomew chuckled, a hollow laugh, 'for what that requires is bravery, which we have discovered, I lack.'

Richard ran down the stairs, meeting Bethany by the morning room door.

'How is he?' she asked.

'He'll live if we can find a way to smuggle him out of here and away, to God knows where.' He looked at her and placed his hands on her shoulders. 'I'll not lie to you, Bethany. He's run away from the army. We have to help him for Mother and Father's sake, but I'm ashamed of what he has done.' Richard kissed her cheek. 'What a family you are to marry into.'

She smiled. 'We had better act quickly,

Richard. Have you a plan?'

'Richard! Richard!' His mama appeared at the top of the stairs. 'Are we having our own private performance? Why wasn't I informed? I should have dressed for it.'

Richard looked at his mother with open despair. Neither had realised that she was up again.

'Ma'am, why should you think we are having a performance here?' Bethany asked, as she walked over to her.

'Well, that actor fellow is standing in our courtyard.' She looked at Richard and smiled. 'Tell me, Richard, can you act or juggle?'

Richard stood there and sighed deeply. 'No, Mama, I cannot, but I suggest you go back to bed as he merely requires assistance with his wagon.'

'Shame, Richard, you should try.' Her eyes were a little watery, and she sniffed before adding, 'I think Bartholomew could, if he weren't a soldier already. He'd make an excellent actor.' She looked from one amazed face to the other, and a little smile appeared.

Richard leapt up the stairs to her. 'Ma, you are a genius!'

'I know, dear!' she said simply, and returned quietly to her bedchamber.

'Bethany, I'll find him some everyday clothes, you stop that wastrel in the courtyard. Tell Henry to fix the wagon and bring it back here.'

She ran to the courtyard and saw the man idly leaning against the stable doorway.

'Henry, Mister Richard wants you to fix the wagon and return it here as soon as possible.' She looked at the actor, who had smiled at her when he recognised Bethany. 'Your presence, sir, is requested indoors.' She turned and he followed her.

'If the lady wishes it, then I obey.'

She glanced back at him, his manner so smooth, so fickle. He never stopped acting. Kezzie had been a little fool, but she could see the similarity between Adam and Bartholomew. They should work well together.

11

In the privacy of her own cottage Sarah turned to Kezzie and Jake. 'You'll be wed!'

'Yes, of course,' Jake replied, and Kezzie nodded her agreement.

'Good. You'll live here?' she looked at Jake.

Kezzie watched her life being organised for her, and swallowed.

'Yes, Mrs Wright,' Jake said politely, 'If that is agreeable to you.'

Sarah looked pointedly at Kezzie, who shifted uneasily. 'Very,' she answered., 'You've been very fortunate, my girl!'

Kezzie's bottom lip trembled a little, and Jake put a protective arm around her shoulder, his gaze not wavering from Sarah's, as he cradled the child protectively.

'You shall both call me, Mama. We are family now.'

Jake smiled broadly and Kezzie nodded. There was nothing for her to say. She was back at home.

* * *

Richard came into the hall where Adam had been told to wait.

'I need you to do what you do best,' Richard said abruptly to him. The man's calm arrogance riled Richard, who could not abide wastrels, but he would provide another fellow spirit with a life-line.

'Act?' Adam said, sarcastically.

'No, I want you to hide someone. You have a knack of being invisible whilst being glaringly conspicuous in what you do, but this time you have a purpose. You will train them to do as you do, and create a new person out of a fellow . . . wastrel. I shall pay you fairly for your inconvenience and you will leave messages every two months as to your whereabouts at a given address in London.'

Richard was followed down the stairs

by a much changed Bartholomew, dressed plainly and simply in normal day clothes.

Bethany looked up at him and thought how ordinary he was without his uniform to hide behind. Even his stance seemed to diminish, as if he was exposed as an ordinary person, nothing to hide behind — like a uniform.

'What if I do not wish to do as you wish, sir?' Adam asked calmly.

'Then you will answer questions at the assizes as to the kidnapping of a young girl, the abuse of the same and how you deserted her in a country village, where there are plenty of witnesses who saw you slope off without a by your leave,' Richard replied.

'You really are quite abrupt, sir. You lack refinement and are a man of 'honour', unlike Bartholomew here.' Adam grinned broadly. 'You did well to escape, Bart. You must be getting more daring these days.'

Bartholomew held out an arm to Adam. 'Glad you made it too.' Bartholomew greeted him like an old friend, and then turned towards Richard. 'How did you know?' he looked genuinely surprised.

Bethany looked on in awe. No wonder they were so alike. 'You both deserted?' she shook her head in disbelief. 'So very alike!'

'No, my dear sweet child!' Adam's manner caused Richard to clench his fists, and Adam changed his approach to Bethany. 'I did not desert; I was unfortunately injured and was discharged.'

'Shot in the foot, no doubt,' Richard answered bitterly. 'Say goodbye to your mother, Bartholomew, then leave us. You'll know how to send word and I shall leave limited funds available by our usual offices in London. If you use them up too quickly, do not come back for more, there will be none available. Make of your life what you can, Bart, this is your last chance whilst you still have one!' Richard took Bethany's hand.

'I'll wait for the wagon outside, Bart. Don't be long. They'll arrive here soon enough.' Adam bowed slightly to

Bethany and casually walked out of the building.

Bartholomew nodded. 'I do appreciate this, little brother.' He looked Richard in the eye. Richard did not reply.

Bethany saw him run up the stairs two at a time. 'He could have been someone to make his parents proud of him,' she said quietly.

'Like what, a hero? The man's a coward to the core.' He placed an arm around her shoulders and squeezed her to him.

'No, someone like you, I was thinking.'

He kissed her tenderly then whispered, 'Hold on to that thought. Come, let us see them off, then we can celebrate.'

Bartholomew composed himself before slipping into his mother's bedchamber. She was lying on her bed, her breath shallow and her fragile body quite still. 'Mama, do you sleep?' he asked quietly.

'How can I, boy, with you all catewauling?' she said simply, as she lay there staring at the ornate plasterwork on the ceiling. 'You've been a naughty boy, Bartholomew. Haven't you?'

'I know, I've not been completely honest. Mother, please don't tell Father. His heart is not strong and he may not take it too well.' Bartholomew stood with one finger placed against the palm of her small hand. He kissed her cheek.

'No, you are quite correct, he's not that strong. It appears to be a family failing.' She looked at him through tired grey eyes.

'Richard turned out to be reliable, Mama. You have him here where you've always wanted him, but then he bears no likeness to either me or Father, does he?' Bartholomew held her hand. 'In fact, when he stood next to the man, James, in the square, there was a striking resemblance to him in stance and profile.'

'No, he doesn't look or behave like either of you, thank God.' She looked at him and her mouth curled into a smile at one side. 'You wicked boy.'

'You'll break his heart if my suspicions are true, Mama. He has fallen in love with his sister. Nasty!' She stared at him, holding his gaze.

'Even if the dregs of your brain were actually thinking straight for once in your futile life, Bartholomew, she is adopted and therefore not of James' blood.'

'Lucky Richard,' Bartholomew whispered.

She closed her eyes and he stepped back. 'Come back for Christmas dinner, Bartholomew, and bring your friend with you. I do enjoy Yuletide so.'

'Yes, Mama,' he said. 'Of course, you have my word.'

He left her, but he heard her say one more comment before he closed the door.

'Whatever that is worth . . . ' Her words seemed to hang in the air for a moment before he clasped the door firmly shut.

The wagon moved off and Richard and Bethany dutifully waved it on its way. 'Do you hate him, Richard?' Bethany asked as they returned to the morning room.

'Hate, no. Disappointed, yes. I'll miss him, because I used to think he was fun. He always had a carefree attitude, but now, not to care about anything but yourself is something I cannot admire in a person.'

'What do you admire in a person, then?'

He swept her up into his arms and answered simply, 'You.'

THE END

We do hope that you have enjoyed reading this large print book.

Did you know that all of our titles are available for purchase?

We publish a wide range of high quality large print books including:
Romances, Mysteries, Classics
General Fiction
Non Fiction and Westerns

Special interest titles available in large print are:
The Little Oxford Dictionary
Music Book, Song Book
Hymn Book, Service Book

Also available from us courtesy of Oxford University Press:
Young Readers' Dictionary
(large print edition)
Young Readers' Thesaurus
(large print edition)

For further information or a free brochure, please contact us at:
Ulverscroft Large Print Books Ltd.,
The Green, Bradgate Road, Anstey,
Leicester, LE7 7FU, England.
Tel: (00 44) **0116 236 4325**
Fax: (00 44) **0116 234 0205**

Other titles in the
Linford Romance Library:

TWISTED TAPESTRIES

Joyce Johnson

Jenna Pascoe is a Cornish fisherman's daughter. When her parents receive news that her mother's sister, aunt Olive, is coming home to England from Italy, they refuse to acknowledge her. Family secrets resurface and Jenna's initial delight turns to dismay. However, Olive and her family turn up at their home, and Jenna meets her handsome cousin Allesandro. How will the families resolve their differences — and how will cousins, Jenna and Allesandro cope with their growing feelings for each other . . . ?